The Mistreatment of Zora Langston

Lisa W. Tetting

This book is a work of fiction. Names, characters, places, and incidents are the product of the author's imagination or are used fictitiously. Any resemblance to actual locales, or persons, living or dead, is coincidental.

ISBN: 978-0-9961429-0-8
Art & Illustration by Monica Gibbs

To the love of my life **Douglas Tetting**.
You are my light in a world of darkness.

A special thank you to my mom, Mrs. Thelma Wright for instilling in me a great work ethic and a positive sense of self worth.

I would also like to thank Ashley and Jen with A.K. Clark Editing for their excellent editing, and Monica Gibbs Graphics for creating the beautiful book cover.

1979

Chapter 1: Daddy Leaves

Hi, my name is Zora Langston, and I am 9 years old. I am from a small town in North Carolina called Goldsboro, where life is slow and the people are good. I live on Beech Street with my parents and my older brother and sister. Today is the worst day of my life and I just need it to be over as quickly as possible. I can't believe my daddy, Barry Langston, left me all alone. He knew my mom hated me and my grandma lives too far away to help. Why would he just abandon me like that? I wanted to go with him, and my heart hurt so much.

I screamed at the top of my lungs, "Daddy! Daddy, come back!" My family was standing at his grave site waiting for the preacher to finish his speech. My mom called it a eulogy, but it seemed like a very long and boring speech from someone who didn't even know my daddy. Daddy always took me to the Church of Christ on Sundays, but this preacher was from the Baptist church my mom attended with my older sister and brother.

"Somebody shut that girl up," my mom said. "She's embarrassing the whole family. Acting so ghetto."

My sister Queenie chimed in, "Doesn't she know that dignified people bury people in silence and with pride? Who ever heard of a child asking her daddy to come back from death?"

It seemed like my brother was lost or numb because he never said a word. This was odd for Big Willie because he always had something to say. He was never without a smooth line or a quick comeback. I guess he was mourning like I was. My mom and sister acted like the only thing they cared about was what everyone would say about their dresses, hair, and make-up. My sister could not wait to be seen in the limo, and I overheard mommy talking to her friends about how nice she was burying my daddy.

"Barry is going to be laid out in the finest suit money can buy" she said. "Oh and that casket, it's the best that they had; mahogany wood with silk lining. He is going out in style, only the best for my husband!"

All of this talk when she knew good and well that daddy would have a fit if he saw the funeral bill. My daddy hated to waste money and he always said, "When I go, just put me in my Sunday suit and a pine box. No need in putting money in the ground. Use it for my baby's education." Of course that fell on deaf ears with Mrs. Teresa Jones Langston!' She was always decked out from head to toe. The baddest lady on our block, according to Mr. Samuels at the corner store. He was always telling people how fine my mom was and what kind of designer clothes she was wearing. I swear he was trying to make a move on Mommy, and now that daddy was gone I wonder how long it will take him to move into our house. Mommy tried to hide it, but she loved the attention he gave her and I saw them holding hands one day. She swore me to secrecy and threatened me within an inch of my life, but I told daddy anyway. He never said a word to her, but I knew it hurt him.

The day my daddy died, I was sitting on the front porch waiting for mommy to unlock the door. I waited for her to pick me up after school, but she never came. Since we walked home the same route every day, I knew my way home. Queenie and Big Willie had afterschool activities and never walked with me. Queenie was a

2

cheerleader and would never be seen with a dork like me. Big Willie was the star of the basketball team, and he was always on the court playing. He would eat and sleep there if Mommy would let him.

My daddy had a heart attack after coming home from work early to let me in the house. A neighbor called him at work to let him know I was sitting outside and couldn't get in. When he arrived I was so happy to see him because I was starving. As we entered the house there were funny noises coming from upstairs. He told me to make myself a snack and he would be right back. When he went upstairs he caught my mommy and Mr. Samuels in the bed together. I was in the kitchen making a peanut butter and jelly sandwich when something told me to go upstairs. As I reached the top stair, I heard Daddy yelling and Mommy was crying, "Please, Barry, don't hurt him!" "Hurt him!" Daddy said in a low voice, almost a whisper. His face went pale and he was shaking. The next thing I knew, Mr. Samuels was running past me in his socks with his ding-a-ling swinging everywhere. Then I saw my daddy clutch his chest and fall to the ground. He looked weak as I rushed to his side. He had enough time to say, "I love you, Zora," before my mommy snatched me up and said, "Get your ass downstairs and you better not say a word to anybody about what you saw." As she was pulling me away, I saw his eyes go dead and then his body went limp. Daddy died there on the floor, and that bitch never even called for help. I never really liked my mom, but after that day I hated her! She killed the love of my life and then stole his final moments with her selfishness. I could never forgive her, and if she thought I was going to keep her secret, she had another thought coming. I was just waiting for the right moment to expose her!

As they lowered my daddy into the ground I tried to jump into the hole, but my Grandma Rose stopped me. She locked on to my arm and refused to let me go. I was screaming and crying because I did not want him to go. She just held me in her arms like she always did and attempted to comfort me. My mom could not be bothered. I was making a scene, and she could never be around that sort of behavior. She took my brother and sister and went to the limo. Grandma Rose said, "Now, baby, you can't go with your daddy. I know you love him, but he's not in that box. Daddy is in heaven, and it would make him so very sad to know you were acting like this. I know it hurts, but you must get yourself together, wipe your face, and then come to the limo. OK, baby?"

Grandma Rose always knew how to say the right thing at the right time. I calmed myself down and told her that I was alright. "Thank you Grandma Rose. I just want to say goodbye, and I will be right there. I promise. I won't try to jump in again."

"Alright, baby. Just hurry up now because you know how your mama is."

"I'll be right there." "OK, I will be in the limo if you need me."

As Grandma Rose walked away, I turned my attention back to my daddy's grave. The men were just about to shovel dirt on top of him when I asked them if I could do it. Something inside of me said "You have to do it. Don't let these strangers put dirt on him." The man handed me the shovel and I put the first bit of dirt on the casket. It made a loud thud, and it stung me. The tears started flowing like a river, but I forced myself to continue. I was working so hard at putting the dirt in that hole that I never even heard my mom come up behind me. By the time I realized what was happening she was slapping me across the face and snatching the shovel out of my hands. When she slapped me dirt got all over her dress which enraged her. "I can't believe your stupid ass is acting like this. You got the whole town looking at me like I raised some type of fool. And you have the nerve to get that cemetery dirt on my new designer dress." She was fuming and talking in a voice just loud enough for me to hear, but no one else. "If you don't get your black ass in this car so we can go home, you are going to need your own grave."

When I got into the limo, Grandma Rose reached out for me, but my mom quickly blocked her. "Old woman, you need to stop babying this girl. She was out of control, and I am not going for her bullshit today." Grandma Rose cleared her throat, but decided this was not the time to argue. She just reached right over my mom, and pulled me with great force onto her lap. She held me tight like she used to do when I was a baby. I put my face on her chest and cried until my tears ran dry. I wanted to cry more, but nothing would come out. Grandma Rose said, "It's ok baby, sometimes God dries up our tears, because he can't bear to see us in so much pain." That made sense to me because the preacher said God loves us and wants the best for us. All I knew was I needed God now more than ever because Grandma Rose was leaving to go back to Virginia in the morning, and Mommy was looking for revenge on me for ruining her dress. I swear she was angrier with me than she was sad about my daddy being dead.

As we walked into our house, I felt a cold chill come over me. I knew I was going to catch hell from Mommy and Queenie. Maybe Big Willie would take pity and take up for me. Yeah right, all he cared about was basketball. I would be on my own as soon as we dropped Grandma Rose off at the bus station. My best bet was to get out of her sight and stay hidden. That way she would not have all the built up anger she usually had for me. Maybe being in a house full of people, and the tasty food from her church friends would put her in a good mood. She sure wasn't mourning! She was good at fronting, though. She would be laughing and running people down, but as soon as someone mentioned Daddy, she acted all sad. "Teresa, I am so sorry for your loss," some lady Mommy knew said. Queue the tears… Mommy could have won one of those awards that the actresses got on TV. She was secretly happy Daddy was dead, but she had to act like she was mourning when people were around.

I decided to hide in the corner of the kitchen where there was a window seat. It had curtains around it so when I closed them nobody could see me. It was the place that Daddy always sat and read to me from his favorite books. That was one of my best memories of my daddy. He was a lover of books, and read all of the time. In fact, he named me after his favorite writer, Zora Neale Hurston. Every Saturday, when my mom and sister were at the beauty shop, Daddy would grab his favorite book, "Their Eyes Were Watching God" and we would sit in that corner and read. I did not understand everything that he read to me, but I loved the story. Daddy told me that true love was the best gift I could ever give someone, and that is what that book was about. He said Mommy was the love of his life, and no matter what she had done to hurt him, he would always love her. His face always looked dreamy when he talked about my mom. I couldn't figure out why he would love such a witch like her. She was mean and nasty to him, and because I was his sidekick, I felt her wrath, too. Daddy always said, "Your mama was not always like this. She used to be fun and free." She was the most beautiful woman he had ever seen.

As I sat in that nook, hiding behind the curtains, I heard all of the people coming and going. They were like vultures at a buffet. "I wonder if Barry left me anything in his will," one lady said. Some other chick was gossiping about Daddy's life insurance, "I heard he had a million dollar policy." Then I heard something I knew would change my life forever. My Auntie Jen was talking to her friend; she said, "You know he wasn't Queenie and Big Willie's daddy anyway. My sister was playing his ass like a fiddle. She was in it for the money." Her friend said, "Nooo girl, I didn't know that. What about the little girl?" "Oh you talkin' bout Zora," my auntie chimed in. "Child, yeah, he's her father. Just look at her with that dark skin. She is ugly as sin just like her Barry. Why you think Teresa can't stand her ass? She reminds her of Barry so much that Teresa wants to just beat the shit out of her on sight." Both of them walked off laughing.

What did she mean? Queenie and Big Willie were not my daddy's children? Did Daddy know about this? How could that evil woman do this to him? Since she hates me so much, will she kill me now? I want her to kill me so that I can be with my daddy. Before I could finish that thought, I heard two men talking about Mommy and Mr. Samuels. "Man you know he was up in here getting that ass when Barry caught them," said one guy. "Damn, that's just wrong. I would have killed that fucker if it was me." The other man said. "I guess my man Barry's heart gave out before he could get that bastard. You know he's the oldest kids' daddy don't you?" the first man exclaimed. "Everybody's been talking about that since Barry died. That bitch is lucky it wasn't me. I don't care how fine she is, I wouldn't be raising no other man's children, and they still fuckin'." The first man then said, "Man, let's get out of here, we paid our respects to Barry, but I don't even want to see her. She is a low- down, dirty tramp."

I couldn't believe my ears. Had daddy known that Mr. Samuels was Queenie and Big Willie's daddy? How could he still love such a horrible woman? True love must hurt more than I realized. Daddy was a saint to put up with such a woman, and still love her after everything she did. Sorry, but I am not a saint, and I will get her back for everything she ever did to my daddy.

As I was lying on the window seat thinking about everything that I overheard, I somehow drifted off to sleep. I woke up to my mom calling my name. "ZORA! Where the hell are you? ZORA!!! I swear I am going to skin you alive when I find you." Since I did not want Mommy to find my special place that I shared with Daddy, I decided to slide down on the floor, and crawl out the back door. Once I was outside, I climbed my favorite tree, and pretended that I was up there the whole time. When Big Willie found me, he teased, "You are in some kind of trouble, girl. Mommy has been looking for you everywhere. She is fire hot. Mommy, I found her!" "Where was she?" screamed Mommy. "She was in the back yard up in the willow tree." "Child, haven't I told you a million times to stay out of that tree? I guess you can't help it since you look just like a monkey. I guess it's in your nature." I felt the rage welling up in me. I was not ugly, and I did not look like a monkey. I usually let her talk to me any kind of way, but not this time. Did she forget that she killed my daddy, and I was there watching her and Mr. Samuels running around naked on that day?

"I am not a member of the primate species and I am not ugly! Just because you're high yellow you think you are better than me, but you are the one who is ugly!"

I thought her head was going to pop off of her neck. Her face turned bright red, and she looked at me with fire in her eyes. She started cursing and screaming at me like I had never seen. She jumped on me, and started wailing on my head. Instead of backing down I started laughing which only fueled her fire. It got so bad that a large crowd grew on the street, and a neighbor had to pull her off of me. Mission Accomplished! I wanted her to lose her cool, act like the street whore she was, and have witnesses from the neighborhood. I would take the beating, lose blood, and deal with a black eye and busted lip if it made her look bad. People were going to be talking about this for days, maybe weeks, and it was not a good look for her. People knew she was pretending to mourn my father, and now she was beating me in front of the entire neighborhood. She fell right into my trap.

Chapter 2: Here Comes Mr. Samuels

The morning after Daddy's funeral, I woke up very confused. I was happy that I got Mommy to beat me in front of the entire neighborhood, but I was worried. Would she feel free to kick my butt whenever she wanted now? Would the sight of me enrage her to the point that she would actually kill me? What about Mr. Samuels, would she wait to move him in, or would it be right away? Grandma Rose was leaving today, and I would have nobody. It didn't take long for my questions to be answered. As soon as she saw me, my mom started grinning. She was proud of the job she did on my face yesterday. I had a black eye, and my lip was swollen, and I was sore as the devil. "I bet your little ass will think twice before pissing me off again," she screeched. "That won't be hard to do," I mumbled under my breath. Thank goodness she didn't hear me.

"Hurry up and get ready to take your grandmother to the bus station. You don't have time to eat" she called to me as I was trying to get the cereal box off of the top of the refrigerator. I was hungry, but I dared not make her mad this early in the day. As soon as we said goodbye to Grandma Rose I knew I was in for another beating. Mommy thought she found a new way to control me, and she was eager to test it. I would have to be smart about making her angry, and would try to be sure there was an audience whenever she lost her cool. People loved to talk, and eventually the child welfare would come to remove me from her house. I wanted out in the worst way, and since I was too young to get a job, I would have to rely on the government to save me. On the way home I decided I would be as still as a church mouse so she would forget I was there. My plan was short-lived because that darnn Queenie just had to start in on me. "What's wrong with you Zora?" she exclaimed. "I know you are sad to see your best friend in the world go. What kind of 9 year old has a best friend in their 70s?" Queenie laughed. I tried my best to ignore her, but when she started talking about my daddy, I jumped all over her. "Your daddy ain't, here to save you, and it's gonna be hell on earth for you. Right, Mom?" "Don't say "ain't" Queenie," was all my mommy could say. She was a stickler for using proper English unless she was mad. "What's wrong, little Zora? You miss your daddy? He was a rich bum anyway. He always stank when he came home, and I never liked him. If it wasn't for you he would have left a long time ago, and my real daddy could have come to live with us." That was it, I felt my skin turn hot and I could not just sit there, and let her pick on me and talk mess about my daddy. I wanted to scratch her eyes out, but just as I went to reach for her, my brother stepped in. "Well he was a lot nicer than our real daddy. At least he was there to help raise us. He loved us, and we saw him every day. I have to go to the corner store just to get a glimpse of my own father. That man doesn't care about us."

I was shocked! Did Big Willie just take up for my daddy? Wait, how did he know that my daddy wasn't his daddy? If he and Queenie knew, that meant Daddy knew. I guess everybody was in on this family secret except me. I want to know how Barry Langston, a fine man who was a great catch for any woman, could fall in love with such a horrible woman like my mom. Did she work a root on him? I bet that's what happened. She needed some poor fool to take care of her and her children so she tricked daddy into drinking her period blood. Once he did that he was trapped, in love with her forever. I heard some older ladies in our neighborhood talking about voodoo and working roots on people a while back. They said that if a woman wanted a man to fall in love with her, and she is not a good catch, all she had to do was trick him into drinking or eating some of her period blood. They told this lady to catch some in a container when she went to the bathroom, and then put it in the man's food. In order to hide the smell and taste, she should make a red sauce like for spaghetti. If the lady could not get him to eat her food, then she must slip it in a drink. That was the nastiest thing I had ever heard! I always thought those old ladies were crazy, but after that day I never wanted to eat spaghetti again. That must be how Mommy did it because Daddy loved spaghetti and meatballs.

As soon as we arrived home Mommy started in, "Zora, I am not playing with your ass today. I need you to get upstairs and start cleaning. Start with the bathroom and don't stop until this entire house is clean. When I say clean, I mean clean. Your brother and sister will do their rooms, and you will take care of the rest. And don't forget to put clean sheets on my bed!" I did not feel like fighting with her today so I did as I was told. It took most of the day, but I had that house sparkling clean. Maybe she would be happy for once and let me be. Just as I sat down with a big glass of ice water she said, "Zora I want you to cook dinner tonight. I'm tired." I couldn't believe it; she had the nerve to say she was tired when she had been on the phone gossiping with her friends all day while I cleaned the house, including her bedroom. *This woman is crazy, I thought to myself.* "I want steak, baked potatoes, and salad. Oh yeah, don't forget my cornbread! I got to have my cornbread. Be sure you make enough for five, we're having company," she sang as she went upstairs to get ready.

Company? Who would be so rude as to invite themselves to dinner the day after we buried our daddy? I did not dare ask her, but about an hour later I found out. In he walked like he owned the joint. His straight black hair was slicked back, and he was wearing some suit that he got at the thrift store. To make matters worse, he smelled like bug spray. Mr. Samuels was the creepiest man I had ever known. I always hated going to the store where he worked because he gave me goose bumps. I could never understand why I was so uncomfortable around him, but he gave me the creeps. Now he was in my house, and I had to feed him, smile at him, and act as if he was welcome. I hated him just as much as I hated Mommy. If it had not been for them, my daddy would still be here with me. They couldn't even let Daddy's body turn cold. I mean it hadn't even been a whole day, and he was sitting in Daddy's chair like it was his all along. "Hi there, Zora," he greeted me as if we were old friends. He was grinning so hard I could see all of his cavities. "Hi Mr. Samuels," I dryly replied. As we sat at the dinner table eating a meal that I prepared, I became sick. Watching this joke of a man sitting at the head of the table, where my daddy once sat, was too much for me. I began to feel the sweet water well up in my mouth. I tried as hard as I could to stop it, but nature took over, and I hurled all over the table. Deep inside I was laughing because this man did not deserve to be here eating food that my daddy paid for. On the outside I pretended that I was deathly ill, even though I felt better immediately after I threw up. "Oh my God, I can't believe this nasty girl has ruined such a lovely dinner. John, I worked so hard to make you such a nice dinner, and she has ruined it," Mommy pretended. "Leave the girl alone, Ree Ree," he said. "She can't help it if she's sick. Let her go lie down, and I'll go out and get us some dinner." "Alright baby," Mommy chimed. "Zora, get yourself cleaned up, and then go to bed. I'll deal with you later." As I was walking towards the stairs I heard Mr. Samuels say, "Baby, you got some money for dinner? I just need about $30 - $40." Mommy said, "Sure, baby, let me get my purse."

I don't know what made me sicker; the fact that he was already scheming money from Mommy or that they were calling each other baby. Was I the only one in the world that thought it was too soon for them to flaunt their love in front of my family? Especially since it was their affair that caused such turmoil. And when did he start calling Mommy "Ree Ree?" She has never liked to be called anything other than Teresa or Mommy. Had she lost her mind?

The next morning I woke up to the most annoying laughter I had ever heard. Mr. Samuels was downstairs, sitting in Daddy's recliner, wearing only his drawers, laughing at the TV while Mommy was prancing around in her night-gown making him breakfast. Did this broke-down pimp sleep here? That was it! She was letting that fool move in here, and it had only been two days! I couldn't believe what was going on. I had to get out of here! I ran down the stairs and straight out of the door so fast Mommy did not have a chance to stop me. I heard her calling me, but I just kept running.

I ended up at the cemetery, the only place I really wanted to be. I found my daddy's grave, and I sat there for hours talking and crying. I was so wrapped up in my talk with Daddy that I never heard the lady come up behind me. "Excuse me, dear," the lady said. I was so startled that I almost jumped to my feet. "I'm sorry, didn't mean to scare you. I was just wondering if your name was Zora." "Yes ma'am," I replied. "My name is Zora. How did you know that?" "I knew your father," she said. "My name is Vivian Smalls, and your father was a very nice man. I am sorry for your loss." "Thank you, ma'am," I said with tears in my eyes. "You miss him, don't you?" she asked. "With all my heart," I whispered as tears streamed down my face. I didn't know why, but there was something about this lady that made me trust her. She had a kind face, and she seemed nice. The only adults that were ever nice to me were Daddy, Grandma Rose and my teacher Mrs. Myers. Mrs. Smalls informed me that my daddy was worried that something would happen to him, and he wanted to be sure that I was taken care of. She said she was a lawyer, and it was her job to look out for my best interest. Daddy had hired her to manage my money until I was old enough to know how to do it myself. She stated Daddy left me a big inheritance, and she was something called an executor. I had no idea what that was so I called her my Fairy God mother. Mrs. Smalls laughed when I said that, and I think she liked it a lot. She gave me something she called a business card and told me to put it somewhere safe. I should use the phone number on it to contact her if I needed anything, and she made me promise not to tell my mom about her. "She'll find out about me soon enough," she said. Thank you, Daddy, you always know what I need!

As I walked back home, I felt calm and relieved. I knew that Mommy was in for a fight, and I now had a friend to help me out. By the time I reached the front porch it was 3 o'clock in the afternoon. I had been gone for 7 hours, and Mommy was hopping mad! "Where have you been, girl?" she demanded. "I know you heard me calling you this morning. You better get in here, and start cooking dinner. I had to make breakfast and lunch, and I refuse to cook anymore today." I just walked past her as if she wasn't there. I knew better than to look her in the eyes. That usually set her off, and I would never hear the end of it. I went to the kitchen, washed my hands, and looked in the fridge to see what we had to cook. I decided fried chicken, mashed potatoes, and green peas with biscuits would be on the menu tonight.

As I began to peel the potatoes, Mommy came into the kitchen to see what I was doing. I could tell she wanted to fuss about something so I made it a point to do everything perfectly. She loved fried chicken and would never argue with me that mashed potatoes, green peas, and biscuits did not compliment the meat. I even made iced tea just the way she liked it with a bag of sugar. Not really, but she loved it sweet! Since she couldn't find anything to get on me about, she decided to get a glass of tea and left the room. Life would be peaceful tonight because she would have her favorite meal, and she had her favorite man. After dinner, I should be able to escape to my room to think about my future.

At the dinner table, that night, we sat down as one big happy family with Mr. Samuel playing the new daddy. I hated seeing him sitting at the head of the table, but I knew to hold my tongue. Everyone chowed down on my meal, and they were all very happy. Queenie was especially excited to finally have her daddy at the table instead of mine. I learned the reason she never got along with my daddy was because she always longed for hers. I guess she thought she would be betraying Mr. Samuels if she let any feelings of love for my daddy seep into her heart. Big Willie could take Mr. Samuels or leave him. Daddy always took time out to play sports with Big Willie, so they got along well. I think he missed Daddy like I do, but was afraid to let it show. Mommy was so very happy to have her man, as she called him, sitting there with his family after all these years. She made my skin crawl. "Zora, you sho' put your foot in this meal," Mr. Samuels exclaimed. I don't know when I've ever had better fried chicken. That must be your gift in life." I didn't say a word, just kept on eating. Mommy said, "Girl, are you so stupid that you can't take a compliment? You better say thank you to your new daddy." Now why on earth would she say that to me knowing that I just buried my daddy? The rage built up in me, and I could not contain it. "He's not my new daddy, you whore! I can't believe you moved him in here acting like my daddy never existed! YOU MAKE ME SICK!" I was screaming at the top of my lungs. She just had to go and ruin my peaceful night. "I hope you choke on a chicken bone," I screamed as I ran up the stairs. I heard my mom yelling, but I did not care what she was saying. Then I heard Mr. Samuels say, "Honey, give her some time. She just lost her dad. It can't be easy for her. Just let her be." That seemed to calm her down for the moment. I was not sure why that old, creepy man was being so nice to me, but I was grateful. I still did not trust him because I knew he wasn't being nice because he was a good person. He wanted something; I just did not know what the cost would be.

Chapter 3: Zora Pays the Cost

Miraculously, I made it through the night without Mommy coming into my room to beat the brakes off of me. If nothing else, Mr. Samuels was good for protection. I knew I had to tread lightly because Mommy was like a firecracker, and it wouldn't take much to set her off. I got out of bed, ran to the bathroom to shower, and got dressed before Queenie could wake up. If she made it in there before me, I was going to be late to school. She always took at least an hour to get ready. I was halfway out of the door when I heard Mommy call down the stairs. I acted like I didn't hear her calling me, and closed the door very gently behind me. I ran up the street, and then started walking in case she looked out of the window. She would think that I really did not hear her because I was so far down the road. When I arrived at school, all of the other kids were whispering and laughing. It seemed like it was directed toward me, but I kept walking like I did not hear them. I was becoming good at ignoring people, and living in my own world. My teacher, Mrs. Myers looked at my face and asked me what happened. I told her a lie, and I think she bought it. "I fell at my daddy's funeral and hit my head on a tree stump." She looked at me like she wanted to cry and said, "Zora, you know you can tell me anything, right?" "I know, Mrs. Myers, but I don't really feel like talking right now," I lied again. All I wanted to do at that moment was tell her that my mommy beat me, and I didn't want to go back home, but I could not bring myself to say anything.

At lunch break the kids in the class had a ton of questions about my daddy. The funny thing was, none of the questions were asked of me. Sheila said, "I heard he died after catching her mama in bed with old man Samuels. Ain't that right?" Linda chimed in, "Didn't they say her mama beat her ass in front of the whole hood?" Everybody burst into laughter. "That's what I know," said Nicole. "I seen the whole thing. Her mama put a hurtin' on her." I couldn't believe all of these stupid kids thought it was funny to watch me get beat to a pulp by my own mother. Not one of them felt bad for me. I knew I was an outsider, but I thought at least one person would have felt bad.

I felt like crying, but Daddy always told me that children were pack animals. They look for weakness and band together to attack you. It was up to me not to show any weakness. I decided the best way to do this was to show some strength. I had to take out the queen herself and everyone else would leave me alone. I walked right in the middle of all those kids and got about an inch from Nicole's face. "If you don't shut your mouth, I'm gonna shut it for you," I threatened. She started to say something smart like she always did, but I did not give her a chance. I punched her dead in her lip! It immediately began bleeding, but I did not care. All of my rage that I had for Mommy was now coming out on her. I wailed on her until I was out of breath, and all I could remember was the janitor pulling me off of her. Mrs. Myers came running and was confused by what happened.

"Zora, what are you doing?" she asked. "Nicole and her friends are telling lies about my daddy, and I won't stand for it," I answered.

"Well this is not the way young ladies handle their disputes. I want you to apologize, this instant." "I'm sorry your mouth wrote a check that your ass couldn't cash," I replied. Everyone started laughing, and Nicole hung her head. She wouldn't be messing with me anymore. Mrs. Myers said, "Nicole, I know you started this, but I can't prove it. Go to the ladies room and get yourself together and then report back to me. Zora, you are going to have to go to the principal's office." I started tearing up then. "I'm sorry, Mrs. Myers. I didn't mean it." "It's too late, Zora. Look at her face. I can't do anything about this now if I wanted to. You have to be punished, but I will talk to Mr. George to see if he can go easy on you because of your circumstances."

Mr. George was a tough cookie. You did not want to go to his office for anything, but fighting was a cardinal sin. I knew I was going to get a stern talking to and then suspended for 3 days. That was the usual punishment for things like this. I was hoping he would take into consideration that I was in mourning, but it was not likely.

Mr. George stood up from his desk when I walked into his office. He must have been about ten feet tall. "Have a seat, young lady," he said sternly. I was so scared of him that my knees began to shake. "What's this I hear about you fighting in my school?" he continued in a deep manly voice. I did not know what to say so I kept quiet. "Now I hear tell that your daddy died last week, so I understand you may be acting out, but I want you to know I will not tolerate any debauchery on my watch. Is that understood?" He was not speaking loudly, but I felt his words vibrating in my chest. "Yes, sir," I said with a shaky voice. "I hope you know that my hands are tied, Zora. If I let you off without punishment, every child in this place will fly off of the handle, and that will not be tolerated. You are suspended for three days." All I could say was, "Yes, sir." Mr. George kept talking, "I will have Mrs. Myers stop by your house with your assignments so you don't fall behind any more than you already have. You are dismissed. Be sure to go straight home and give your mother this paper explaining what happened."

I took the dreaded pink slip from his hand and I ran so fast out of his office I didn't even see Nicole and her mother sitting in the lobby. They were waiting to speak with Mr. George. "There she is mama!" whined Nicole as she pointed to me. "Young lady," she said. "Why did you hit my baby?" I almost stopped, but I knew better than to argue with an adult. I just kept running as she chased after me. I knew I could outrun her so I did not even look back. I heard Mr. George calling after her to see how he could help. I remember thinking she sure got to school fast, and then I realized that she worked at the school as a secretary.

As soon as I walked in the front door I knew something strange was going on. There was music playing and candles were lit. I walked into the kitchen and I saw Mr. Samuels licking whipped cream off of the neighbor lady's boobies. I started laughing and said, "Now what's going on here?" They almost jumped out of their skin! I did not know this lady's name, but I saw her all of the time at the corner store where Mr. Samuels worked. Both of them looked embarrassed and neither of them had on a top. She was still wearing her skirt, but it was up around her waist and her boobies were exposed. He was wearing his boxers and socks. "Y'all nasty, and I'm telling Mommy!" I yelled. "Get out of my house, lady," I screamed. You would have thought I was Mommy the way that woman took off out the door. I swear there was smoke coming from her feet. "And you," I continued, "Just what do you think you are doing? My mommy is going to be furious. You better start packing your stuff now cause when she gets home she is going to kill you." Mr. Samuels looked panicked. "Why are you home? Shouldn't you be in school?" All of a sudden he calmed down and a devious look came over his face. "Listen, Zora, we are friends aren't we? Now let's make a deal. I won't tell your mom that you got in trouble at school if you keep this to yourself." Wait a minute, how did he know I got in trouble at school? Oh yeah, I was holding the pink slip of paper Mr. George gave me. "Mr. Samuels. I don't think you get it," I chimed in. I don't really care if Mommy knows that I got in trouble at school. I am not your friend, and I refuse to make a deal with the devil!" Mr. Samuels' face dropped. Where there was once fear there was now rage. "I tried to be nice, little girl, but your dumb ass don't know when a gift horse is looking you in the face. Now I'm gonna make sure you don't tell her! We gonna have a lot of secrets around here."

At that moment I felt my stomach curl into a big knot. I was scared for the first time. I kept thinking of things he could do to me: lock me in the closet, beat me, set me on fire; the list went on and on. I was not prepared for what he actually had in mind. As I stood there, he started coming closer to me.

As I turned to run, I felt him grab my ponytail. I screamed, but that did not stop him. He smacked me, and I fell to the ground. I tried to get up, but he was standing over me, and I was trapped in the corner. There was no escape, and I knew he was going to kill me. "Stop screaming or I'll slit your throat," threatened Mr. Samuels. "Since you interrupted my little party and made my girl leave, you are going to take her place. Now you're too young to really get down so I'm gonna start you slow. Get on your knees," he demanded. I had no idea what he was talking about. How in the world was I going to take the neighbor lady's place? I don't even have boobies and he was all out of whipped cream. "When you're older you will thank me for showing you how to do this. Open your mouth." I refused to open my mouth because I thought he was going to make me eat something sour. I began shaking because I looked up and saw that his ding-a-ling was sticking straight out in front of him. I thought something was wrong with him. Ding-a-lings are not supposed to stand up by themselves, they are supposed to dangle between boys' legs. "I said open your mouth!" he yelled again as he yanked my head backwards and pinched my nose so I couldn't breathe. I had to open my mouth or suffocate, and I chose to breathe. As soon as I opened my mouth he shoved his thing down my throat. It was salty and I was choking because it was so big. I panicked and tried to get up, but he shoved me back down on my knees. "You are going to learn to give good head, and whenever I need it you will do it." What was he talking about? I didn't know what was going on. All I knew was it was the nastiest thing that had ever had happen to me, and I wanted it to stop. He just kept putting that thing in further and further until I was coughing and gagging. I thought he was trying to kill me. "Relax and it will be easier for you." He started pulling it out, and I thought he was finished, but then he shoved it back in. "Don't use your teeth! Just relax. Yeah, like that." He kept going in and out, in and out faster and faster. I figured that he must really like what was happening because he started moaning and groaning like he did when I listened at Mommy's door. I knew this was wrong and I was very embarrassed that he was doing this to me. All of a sudden he howled and peed in my mouth! I was horrified and tried to spit it out. "No, bitch, you gonna swallow that," he commanded. I felt dirty and nasty, but I did as he told me. His pee tasted gross and it was white. I thought he was some kind of alien because everyone knows pee is yellow. "You just swallowed my baby batter," he bragged. Mr. Samuels was so proud of himself for making me do such a nasty thing. "You gonna be better than your mama when I'm finished with you, girl!" I thought for sure that he was poisoning me. I knew what he did was wrong, but I felt like it was my fault. Why didn't I just agree to his stupid secret? If I had, he never would have stuck that thing in my mouth. As he was talking, I felt sick, and I threw up right there on the kitchen floor. He slapped me across the face and said, "Clean that shit up before your mama comes home, and you better not tell her what we did. You know she hates you, and she will believe anything I say. I'll tell her you tried to have sex with me when I was taking a nap. She will put you out on the streets. If you tell anyone, I will kill you."

As I cleaned the kitchen floor, I saw him watching me. His eyes made me feel dirty and ashamed. I wanted to die, but I had no idea why. He was the one who peed in my mouth, so why did I feel so bad? I wondered how often he would start peeing in my mouth, and why he liked it so much. All I knew is I needed to get out of this house, and I knew just the person to call: Grandma Rose.

Chapter 4: Grandma Rose Goes Greyhound

Mr. Samuels took a nap on the couch, so I decided to go to my room. When I got upstairs I wanted to wash my mouth out, and brush my teeth. I still felt a little sick, and needed to get that taste out of my mouth. When I finished in the bathroom I wanted to call Grandma Rose. I did not want Mr. Samuels to bother me again, so I took the phone from Mommy's room, and stretched the cord into my room. I pushed the dresser against the door so he could not get in, and I called Grandma Rose. "Hello," she answered. I was so happy to hear her voice I almost forgot that I was on the phone, and she couldn't see me. "Hi, Grandma Rose," I whispered. "Hey, baby! What are you doing calling me in the middle of the day?" "Grandma, I need you! I got in a fight today at school, and Mr. George suspended me for 3 whole days. When I got home Mr. Samuels was here with another lady. He got mad that I made her leave, and then he peed in my mouth," I blurted out.

Grandma Rose was very quiet at first, then she said, "What are you talking about, Zora? He peed in your mouth?" I could feel the coldness in her voice. She sounded like a ghost. "Yes, he said that he was going to make me better at giving head than my mom. He stuck his thing in my mouth and peed some white pee." Grandma Rose yelled, "I'm gonna kill that son of a bitch! Zora, where is he now?" she asked. "He's downstairs asleep on the couch," I answered. "I'm in my room with the dresser against the door." Grandma Rose

23

seemed to be choosing her words carefully, "Baby, did he do anything else to you. I mean, did he touch your pocketbook?"

Ever since I was a very little girl, Grandma Rose always told me to take care of my pocketbook, and not to let any boys see it. She was very specific with her instructions about keeping it clean, and smelling good. "No young lady should have a smelly pocketbook," she always said.

"No ma'am," I answered. "He said I wasn't old enough to really get down like that." "Zora, have you said anything to anyone else?" "No ma'am, you were the first person I could think to call for help." Grandma Rose seemed relieved, "Good and make damn sure you don't tell your crazy tail mama. There's no tellin' what she'll do. Listen, this is what we're gonna do."

Grandma Rose went on and on with her plan about how she was going to have me come live with her. One of her conditions was I couldn't say anything to anybody about what happened. She said people would not be nice to me, and that what happened in your home stayed in the home. She planned to purchase a bus ticket that afternoon, and would be at my house by mid-morning. I should go about business as usual, and not say a word to Mommy that she was coming. At all costs I was to avoid being alone with Mr. Samuels. Then she told me to pray. She said that God saw what Mr. Samuels did to me, and He would punish him. My job was to talk to God and tell Him my troubles, and she would be here in the morning. I agreed to her conditions, and hung up the phone. I packed all of my favorite clothes, and then I hid the bag in the back of the closet. Now all I needed was to get through the night. I knew I was going to get my butt handed to me because I was suspended from school, and I was not looking forward to Mommy coming home. I decided to lie down on my bed to take a nap, but every time I closed my eyes, all I could see was Mr. Samuels face as he shoved that thing in and out of my mouth. Since I couldn't sleep, I decided to read. I picked up Daddy's favorite book, and began reading where he and I left off before he died. Before I knew it, I heard Mommy come through the front door.

"John, what the hell are you doing lying there in your drawers?" I heard Mommy yelling. "What if I was the children coming home? You can't lie around like that in this household." "I'm sorry, baby, I was just relaxing on my day off. I didn't see anything wrong with it," he lied. "It's ok, but at least put on your bathrobe. Did Zora make it home from school yet? I need her to run to the store," Mommy asked. "Yeah, I think she's up in her room." "Did she see you like that?" "Oh baby, I don't know. I was sleeping. She don't know what she's seeing anyway." He lied again. "Well, just so we're clear, I don't want you around here in your drawers. Put on some damn clothes. You understand?" Mommy demanded. "Yeah baby, I hear you, damn!" I heard him coming upstairs, so I decided to hide under my bed.

"ZORA!" Mommy yelled. "Get down here, I need you to go to the store," she demanded. I did not want to leave the safety of my room, but I knew I had to. I refused to run into Mr. Samuels in the hallway, so I decided I would let Mommy come to me. "ZORA, I know you hear me, girl," she yelled again. I was frozen. I knew it would make her furious, but I stayed under my bed. Just then I heard her stomping up the stairs. "Zora, open this door," she said as she pushed with all her might. I forgot about the dresser I pushed against the door. "Zora, what's going on in there?" Mommy was able to push her way into my room, and found me cowering under the bed. "Girl, what are you doing? Didn't you hear me calling you? Why are you hiding under the bed?" As I got ready to answer her I saw Mr. Samuels standing in the door with a threatening expression. "I got suspended from school for fighting," I said in a very low whisper. "What did you say? Girl, you better stop mumbling and tell me what's going on," she screamed. I could tell her patience was getting low. "I got suspended from school for fighting," I yelled. She immediately smacked me across the mouth. "Why were you fighting, little girl? I am so tired of you. How many days do I have to worry about you being in my house alone during the day?" she said. "Three" I said with caution. "I don't know what I'm going to do with you." Mommy went on and on about how much of a disappointment I was to her and how she would be glad when I wasn't her problem anymore. She sent me to the store to get food for dinner, and as a part of my punishment I had to cook dinner for every night I was suspended. That was no big deal since I did most of the cooking anyway.

The night went by very slowly, and after dinner I was forced to do Queenie's chore of washing dishes. This was also part of my punishment. I didn't mind because it kept me away from Mr. Samuels, and it also helped the time pass. That night I was afraid that Mr. Samuels would come into my room, so I pushed the dresser against the door again. I knew he could still get in because Mommy was able to earlier, but at least he would make a lot of noise doing so. Maybe Mommy would hear him, and come to my rescue. I know she loves him, but she would not let him hurt me, would she? I was so very tired, but I couldn't sleep. My mind kept going back to what happened earlier with Mr. Samuels. Why had Grandma Rose asked me if he touched my pocketbook? Did that mean what he did to me was sex? I knew it was bad, but I never thought it was sex. What kind of person had sex in their mouth? I always heard the older kids talking about boys sticking their ding-a-lings in girls' pocketbooks. They said you could have a baby that way. Wait a minute: Mr. Samuels said I swallowed his baby batter. Did that mean I could have a baby? I would ask Grandma Rose all of these questions when she arrived in the morning.

The next morning, as Mommy was getting ready for work, there was a loud knock on the door. It was Grandma Rose coming to save me! I opened my bedroom door, ran down the stairs only to discover, there was a policeman at the door. He was tall, and his uniform was neatly pressed. I could see his gun on his hip, and his badge was reflecting the sun. "Good morning, ma'am," he said. "Is this the Langston home?" "Yes it is. How may I help you?" asked Mommy. "I'm sorry to have to inform you, but Mrs. Rose Langston was found dead," he continued. Mommy acted like she was upset, but it was fake. I screamed at the top of my lungs, "Nooooo! She was coming to save me," I broke down in tears. The policeman tried to comfort me when he saw that Mommy was not going to. "It's ok, little one," he said. "Everyone has to die some-time." Mommy did not want him talking to me so she interrupted, "She was very close to Rose. She's my mother-in-law, and my husband just passed away a few days ago. Zora, go upstairs to your room," Mommy said cold-heartedly. The policeman looked at her like she was crazy. "Do you think she will be alright, ma'am? What did she mean that Mrs. Langston was coming to save her?" he asked. "She'll be fine. I'll take care of her. Now what happened to Rose?" The policeman said that Grandma Rose was on the Greyhound bus on her way here, when she suddenly had a heart attack. There were no trained medical professionals on the bus, so she died. Her body had been taken to the local hospital, and we would have to go there to claim it.

After the policeman left, I was distraught. How could Grandma Rose be dead, too? She was the only one who loved me in this world. What was going to happen to me now? Was this my fault because I forgot to pray like she told me?

Chapter 5: Zora Gives In

After Grandma Rose died, I did not want to speak to anyone, not even to God. I just wanted to curl up and die. Nobody cared what I was feeling, so I was able to stay in my room most of the time. Mommy decided not to have a funeral, so I couldn't even say goodbye. She claimed we couldn't afford two funerals in the same month, but that was a lie. She hated Grandma Rose, and had her body burned up and put in a jar before she told my uncle. Because I still had 2 days left on my school suspension, I was afraid Mr. Samuels would start making me give him head again. He already told me I was going to be better than my mommy, so I knew he would do it again. I had to find a way to get out of this house. Mr. Samuels worked just down the street from the house, and he could come home any time he wanted.

As a part of my punishment, Mommy had a long list of chores that I had to complete in the next few days. She made it very clear that I did not have a choice in completing them; it was mandatory! She also reminded me there was no one in the world left to care about me, so she was free to do whatever she wanted. I decided that I did not want to die, so I came up with a plan to survive until I could escape this house. I chose to do as I was told, and keep out of everyone's way until I could find someone to help me. My main plan was to complete the list Mommy gave me, find other ways to please her and avoid Mr. Samuels in the process. I had an escape route all planned out if he came home during the day. The only thing was he had to come home when I was downstairs for my plan to work. If I was doing chores upstairs, I was doomed.

One of the chores on my list was to wash all of the windows in the house. My plan was to start upstairs, and work my way down. It was more likely that I would finish the ones upstairs before Mr. Samuels came home for lunch. When he did come home, I would leave out of the back door, and hide in my favorite willow tree. There were several places to hide in the yard. If that failed, I would go to the front yard, and do the gardening. No way would he bother me outside where all of the nosey neighbors could see. I was almost done with the last upstairs window when I heard keys in the front door. I tried my best to finish that window and hide, but when I turned around he was standing right on top of me. I tried to get away from him, but he was too strong.

"Hey Zora, what are you up to?" he stupidly asked. He was well aware of the list that Mommy gave me. It was only 10:30 am, so why was he home? "I needed a break from the store and said to myself, John, you should go to the house, and give Zora another lesson in giving head." My blood ran cold. Now that I knew what he meant, I most definitely did not want him to put that thing in my mouth again. Before I could try to talk him out of it, he grabbed me and was touching my butt and in between my legs. "No, don't do that, Mr. Samuels!" I screamed. "Shut your mouth, girl, and do as I say," he demanded as he struck me in the face. He took his thing out, and started rubbing it with his hand; up and down he went. Then he grabbed my hand and made me do it. "Spit in your hand and then stroke it," he said. I did what he said, and it seemed to please him. I was tired of being hit, so I gave in. "Now put it in your mouth," he instructed. Mr. Samuels really thought he was doing me a favor by 'teaching' me how to please a man. I was not impressed with his subject matter. "You're getting good at this, little girl. Now, take your other hand and rub my balls; squeeze them lightly, and be careful not to hurt me," he demanded. I was grossed out by the thought of touching those weird looking sacks, and hesitated. He smacked me on the side of my head, and it hurt so bad that I heard ringing in my ears. I started crying, and that made him angrier. "Bitch, stop that damn crying. You're going to do as I say when I say it, or I'm gonna beat the shit out of you. Do you understand? Now stop that blubbering and start sucking." That was it! I could not handle everything that was happening to me all at once, and no longer cared about anything. I decided I would do whatever he told me to do without hesitation. It was as gross as I thought it would be, but I never let him see it on my face. I was learning to keep my feelings inside, and show him what he wanted to see. I started to think of it as a challenge. I did what he wanted, when he wanted, and I never showed my disgust. He liked the fact that he could control me, and he became so excited that he peed again. "I'm coming!" he shouted along with his grunts and groans. This must be the warning I get when he is going to pee. Mr. Samuels told me the last time that I had to swallow it, so I did it this time without being told. He checked to make sure it was all gone. I still felt sick, but I learned to hold it in until he let me up to go to the bathroom. I hated him for doing this to me, and I hated Mommy even more because she allowed him to live here. Now that he was finished with me, he had more instructions. "Damn girl, you getting better. I'm coming home for lunch at 1:00, and I want you to do it again. I expect you to be better the next time. Make sure you brush your teeth, and be ready when I stick it down your throat. I don't want to hear any choking."

After he left, I ran to the bathroom, and threw up. I washed my face, brushed my teeth, and even used some of Mommy's mouth wash. I cried for about 15 minutes, and then I remembered that I had to finish the windows. I was working so hard on those windows that I finished them all before 12:30 pm. I was tired and sweating when I finished, and I needed water in the worst way. As I drank my glass of cold water, I began thinking about my life. Mr. Samuels was a nasty dog, and I was nasty for letting him pee in my mouth. Only dirty girls let a man put his thing in their mouth. That's what Mr. Samuels said when he was doing it. Did this mean I was a prostitute? I was so upset about what was happening to me that I barely saw the policeman walking up the sidewalk. "Good morning, young lady," he said with a smile. It was the same policeman who told us the news about Grandma Rose. I wondered what he wanted because nobody ever just came by to say hello, and I was not a young lady anymore. I was a dirty girl. "Hi, my mommy is not home," I replied. "That's ok, I wanted to talk to you." He must have seen the scared look on my face because he went on explaining, "I was driving by and saw you working on those windows. I wondered why you weren't in school, and decided to stop and see if you needed help." I laughed and said, "You want to help me wash windows?" He laughed too and said, "That must seem like a silly thing to say. What I meant was I was worried about you from the other day, and wanted to check on you." Now what would make him worry about me? I didn't even know this man. Did he want to pee in my mouth too? He's a cop and maybe he is trained to sniff out the dirty girls. "There was just something that bothered me the other day, and I wanted to ask you a question. What did you mean when you said your grandma was coming to save you?" he asked. "Oh that, I was just going to live with her that's all." "So how is that saving you?" I was scared to answer him truthfully, so I tried to avoid his question. "Would you like something to drink?" I asked. "No thank you, young lady. I can see that you are not comfortable talking to me, but I want you to know I am here if you need help. I am going to leave you my card, and you call me when you need me." As I put his card in my pocket, I thought maybe I might still be a young lady since he kept calling me one. Then I heard footsteps on the driveway and poof, there he was: Mr. Samuels. "Zora, what's going on here?" he asked with a tremble in his voice. I jumped involuntarily, and my hands began to shake. The policeman must have sensed something was wrong because he moved in

31

between me and Mr. Samuels. "Can I help you sir?" he asked with authority. "I live here. Can I help you?" Mr. Samuels replied sarcastically. The policeman was not amused, and started to get upset when I touched his arm. "Officer, this is my mommy's boyfriend, Mr. John Samuels, and he moved in after my daddy died." I wanted to tell his business without coming right out and saying it. "I see, well I just stopped by to see if you all needed anything with the recent death of Zora's grandma." Mr. Samuels relaxed a bit and said, "We're fine, but thank you for the concern." Mr. Samuels just dismissed the policeman and said, "Zora, I need my lunch." I reluctantly waved goodbye to the officer with a sad expression on my face. I did not want him to leave because I felt safe from Mr. Samuels when he was around. "See you later, Zora," he said and then whispered, "Don't forget to call me if you need to."

I went inside very slowly trying to avoid what was coming next. "Why the hell was that cop over here?" I could see he was angry, so I tried to take his mind off of the policeman. "I don't know. I was washing the windows, and he just showed up. What would you like for lunch?" Mr. Samuels wasn't going for it. "Don't try to change the subject. Did you tell him anything?" I was scared he would hit me again, so I quickly said, "I did not tell him anything. He was asking about Grandma Rose, and I told him to come back when Mommy was home." That seemed to satisfy him, and he moved on with his lunch. "Hurry up and make me a sandwich so we can get down to business." I had hoped he would have changed his mind after seeing a policeman at our house, but he did not. He meant business, and I was going to have to satisfy him. After he gobbled down the sandwich I made him, Mr. Samuels was ready for action. "I'm still hungry," he growled, "But not for food." What did that mean? I had no idea what he was talking about. How can you feed somebody without food?

"Come here, Zora, and take off your jeans," he commanded. I did not want to, but I could not take being hit anymore today. His blows were ten times harder than Mommy's, and my head was still hurting from earlier. I slowly removed my jeans not knowing what he was going to do. Was this really happening? Was he actually going to stick his thing in my pocketbook? "Girl, hurry up. I don't have all day. Take those panties off, too. I'm going to make you feel real good." As I removed my panties, I began to panic. I didn't want to have a baby, and I sure didn't want to have his baby. "Sit on this chair, and open your legs." I did as I was told and watched as Mr. Samuels got on his knees and began touching me where I pee. What was he doing? Then he put his face down there. He began licking and sucking then he started moaning. I started to feel funny, and I think I peed on myself because it was very wet down there. Mr. Samuels didn't seem to mind. In fact he liked it which made me think he was nastier than I thought. "I want you to cum," he said. I didn't know what he was talking about. Come where? He kept licking and sucking; the more he did it the wetter the chair got. Then something happened that scared me! It started vibrating down there, and it felt very good. I was ashamed that I liked it, and jumped up off of his face. Mr. Samuels began to laugh and said "Aww yeah. That's your first orgasm, and I gave it to you!" He was so proud of himself. He looked like a clown with pee dripping down his chin and a big goofy grin on his face. His normally perfect hair was messed up, and his eyes were big and glossy. I was shocked that my body betrayed me, and I did not know what to do. "Now it's your turn. My johnson is hard as a rock," Mr. Samuels said. "You're still too little to fuck, but you sure can suck," he added. I knew what he wanted, and I gave it to him. He peed fast this time, so I did not have to do it for very long. He drank a glass of water, washed his face and slicked back his hair. Then he went back to work happy and singing. I was very confused and sick. I threw up again, in the kitchen sink this time. I had so many questions to ask, but nobody to answer them. Why did I pee in the chair? I did not want him to touch me, so why did it feel good? Did it mean that I liked him if my body vibrated like that? Will I like it if he does it again? I did not know how I was going to continue living like this. How was I going to face Mommy now that her boyfriend made me pee? Was he my new boyfriend? I didn't want him to be my boyfriend. I just wanted him to leave me alone. All I knew was I had to clean up this kitchen, and then finish that list Mommy gave me. I had to be finished before she got home from work, and I wasn't half-way done. Then I heard a voice in my head. It was Grandma Rose telling me to pray. I had forgotten to pray the last time, and she died, so I decided I had better do like she told me this time. "Please God, I need help! Get me out of here," was all I could think of to say.

Chapter 6: Zora's Inheritance

God must have been waiting for me to obey my Grandma Rose because a little while later there was a knock at the front door. I was still doing my list of chores, and was annoyed that whoever was there was going to get me in trouble. To my surprise, Mrs. Smalls was standing on the front porch with a huge grin on her face. "Good afternoon, Zora! How are you, sweetie?" she asked very cheerfully. I didn't know why, but I felt compelled to throw myself in her arms, and burst into tears. "Oh my goodness, what's wrong?" she said more surprised than concerned. "Mrs. Smalls everything is going wrong. First my daddy died, then Grandma Rose, and now Mr. Samuels is." Just then I caught myself. I almost told her what he was doing to me. He said he would kill me, and Mommy would put me out on the streets for sure. "You poor baby, I did not know about your Grandmother. I am very sorry. Now what is this about Mr. Samuels?" she replied. I did not know if I could really trust her, so I only told her part of it. "Mr. Samuels is living here in my daddy's house. He's only been dead a few days, and Mommy has already replaced him." I didn't exactly lie. I just didn't tell her everything all at once. She was shocked to hear this news. "Oh she has, has she? Don't worry, Zora. I am here to help you. Is your mother home?" "No ma'am, she's still at work. She should be home in about 30 minutes. I have a list of chores to do before she arrives."

"Zora, I went by your school, and spoke with your principal. He says you got into a fight and were suspended for three days. What happened?" she asked cautiously. "Some girls were talking about my daddy, and the way Mommy beat me the day of his funeral. I didn't like what they were saying, so I went to the pack leader, and punched her in the mouth." Mrs. Smalls kind of chuckled and then said, "I see. And what, pray tell, did you mean by your mommy beating you on the day of the funeral?" I got scared. Would Mommy get mad if she knew Mrs. Smalls was here asking questions? Would she beat me even worse than before? She must have sensed my apprehension because Mrs. Smalls said, "Don't be afraid. You can tell me anything. Remember, your daddy sent me to help you. I work for him! It's my job to protect you, but you have to tell me the truth no matter what. OK?"

That's right: Daddy did send her to help me! I have to trust someone, and she's all I have. At that moment, the flood-gates opened, and I told her everything about my short life. She heard about the way Daddy died, how Mommy hated me and beat me just to make sure I did not forget. I told how Queenie and Big Willie were Mr. Samuels' children, and how quickly Mommy let him move in. Then I told her my shameful secret about Mr. Samuels peeing in my mouth, and how he made me pee too. I wanted to tell her it felt good, but I was too ashamed and guilty. I didn't want her to think of me as a dirty girl.

I saw tears in her eyes as I told her my story. Mrs. Smalls seemed like a tough lady, but she looked sick. Just then I heard Mommy's car drive up. Whatever pity Mrs. Smalls had for me came out in disgust for Mommy. "Does she know what her boyfriend is doing to you?" she demanded. "No, the only person I told was Grandma Rose, and she died before she could save me. She was going to take me away from here," I replied. "Well don't worry, Zora, because I am not going to let this continue. This stops right now!" Mrs. Smalls promised.

As she walked up the sidewalk to the house, Mommy looked mad and upset. "Zora, whose car is this out front? I know John better not have nobody in my house." Then she saw Mrs. Smalls. "Who the hell are you?" Mommy demanded. "Zora, get me some ice water," she said without missing a beat. I did as I was told, and I also brought Mrs. Smalls a glass. "Thank you, Zora. That was very thoughtful," Mrs. Smalls said, as I handed her the water. Mommy did not like the fact that some strange lady was being nice to me, so she got mad. "Lady, I asked you a question. Who the hell are you? Don't let me ask you again." Mrs. Smalls chuckled and introduced herself, "My name is Vivian Smalls, and I am an attorney with Barnett, Smalls, and Woods. I represent the estate of Mr. Barry Langston." When Mommy heard that she changed her tune. "Oh, how do you do? I am sorry. I thought you were here to see a friend of mine. Won't you have a seat?" Mommy was now on her best behavior. She wanted to make a good impression because this lady held her future in her hands. What Mommy didn't realize was that Mrs. Smalls was here to save me. God and Daddy had sent her to help me, and get me out of here because that is what I prayed for.

"Mrs. Langston," she continued. "Are you aware that your boyfriend, John Samuels, is molesting your daughter?" Mommy's mouth dropped open, and she turned bright red. "What do you mean molesting? John would never touch his own flesh and blood!" she said defensively. "Oh, I'm sure he wouldn't, but Zora is not his flesh and blood, now is she?" The shit was hitting the fan, and I was the cause of it. Mommy looked at me as if she wanted to kill me. "She's a lying little bitch. My man never touched a hair on her head," Mommy said. "Why did you tell this lady those lies, Zora? Do you think it will stop me from getting my money from your dead daddy? Well, it won't. I was his wife, and the law says I have a right to that money!" "I'm sorry to disappoint you, but Zora was the sole heir to Mr. Langston's estate. All of his assets transferred to her upon his death. Mrs. Rose Langston was listed and the trustee of the estate, but since I was just informed of her recent demise, the secondary trustee is myself! I have specific instructions from Mr. Langston as to how this inheritance can be utilized, and I will not stray from them not one little bit. I will be in control until Zora's 18th birthday, and then she will be able to do as she pleases with the money." Mrs. Smalls let Mommy have it! "Since I am the one with the law degree, let me tell you how this works legally. If something were to happen to me, my law office will take over as the trustee. You, my dear woman, will never get your hands on Zora's money! Mr. Langston was very clear on that matter. This will is iron-clad and uncontestable."

You could have knocked her over with a feather. Mommy started crying and whining, "But I was his wife all those years. I had to sleep with his ugly ass, and I even gave him his precious daughter that he wanted. I was through having children, but no, he insisted on one more. I always hated that little bitch, and now you're telling me she gets all of my hard-earned money?" Mommy was out of her mind. She was saying things out loud that she usually said behind closed doors. I couldn't believe my ears. "Zora owns this house that you are living in. It is my duty to present you with an eviction notice. You have 30 days to vacate the premises, or you will be forcibly removed. In the meantime, if I hear one rumor that you or anyone else has harmed this child, I will personally see to it that you never see the light of day again. Do I make myself clear?" Mrs. Smalls wasn't playing. "Now, Zora would you kindly show me to the telephone so I can call the police and DCS to remove you from your mother's care?" I took her into the kitchen, and she made her phone calls. I was happy and scared all at the same time. Did this mean that Mr. Samuels would leave me alone now? Would Mommy stop beating me? Would I have a normal life like all the other kids at school?

Mrs. Smalls waited for the social worker and the police to come, and then she informed me that I would be staying at her house for a little while. I was excited, but also nervous. Did she have a husband, and would he want to pee in my mouth? What if he thought I was big enough to get down? Luckily I did not have to find out because Mrs.

Smalls was actually Miss Smalls. She was young, but she owned her own 3 bedroom house. She had never been married because she spent most of her time at work. She went to college right after high school, and then to law school. She was much too busy to fall in love and have children. She told me that she loved kids, and eventually she would like to get married, but it just had not happened for her yet. This was a very small town, and there were not that many well-to-do black men around. The ones I knew of were already married. She couldn't possibly like white men, so her best bet would be to move away to a big city where there must be lots of rich black men her age. I was wrong about that, too. She said she had no intention of moving to a big city because she was needed in Goldsboro. She also had a crush on one of her co-workers who was a white man. She made me promise to keep that a secret because it was not acceptable for them to date. Her father would have a fit, and it was against the rules at work. They were not dating, but I could tell she liked him by the way she talked.

The police and the social worker stayed at my house until Mr. Samuels got home from work. Queenie and Big Willie were already upstairs doing their homework, and the social worker had spoken with them. She determined that Mommy was not a threat to them because she loved them. However I would not be safe in her custody, so Mrs. Smalls was awarded temporary custody until we could go to court. When Mr. Samuels arrived at my house that evening he was arrested, and charged with child molestation. The whole neighborhood was watching as the police dragged him out of the house kicking and screaming. He was crying like a scared little boy because he knew what was waiting for him in jail. The word on the street was criminals did not take too kindly to child molesters, and they would really mess him up. I did not take pleasure in the fact that he was going to be hurt like he hurt me. I only wanted him to stop. I did not want him to go to jail, but then Miss Smalls reminded me that if he wasn't punished he would turn around, and do it to some other little girl. When she said that, I was down for him going to jail. No other girl would be hurt because I was being soft-hearted. I would not allow it.

Mommy was crying hysterically when they took Mr. Samuels away. She didn't even cry like that for my daddy when he died. In fact she only cried in public about my daddy, but laughed and rejoiced in private. I believed she would have allowed him to continue his abuse of me if she had found out. She even said to me that I ruin everything she has ever had. She actually thought I wanted Mr. Samuels to touch me. I get sick at the thought of it. Queenie was just as distraught over her father being arrested. She vowed she would get her revenge on me. Big Willie seemed unaffected. I heard him say, "That's what that bastard gets. He never loved us anyway." He was more concerned that his father did not spend time with him than the fact that his father was abusing me. I just thanked God that I didn't have to live there anymore, and there would be no more beatings from Mommy. I will miss her, though. I loved my mom despite the fact that she hated me; I just didn't realize it until now.

Chapter 7: Back to School

After all the drama that went on at my house last night, I was happy that I did not have to go to school today. Miss Smalls got me up and made me breakfast. I was not used to someone serving me. It felt kind of good. While we were eating, she informed me that it was "take a friend to work day" at her job, and I was going to be her friend. I was excited because nobody had ever chosen me to be their friend before. She seemed like she really cared what happened to me, and I was grateful. She also said since we were friends, I could call her Vivian. I felt funny calling an adult by her first name, so I asked if she had a nick-name. She did not have a nickname, but decided that I should call her Vivi. I liked that a lot better because I did not feel as if I was showing disrespect. It also made me feel like she was actually my friend.

We had to dress up because Vivi said her office dress-code was professional. I did not know what that meant, so I wore a dress that I usually saved for church. I combed my hair and used my special ribbons to make sure I looked good. I wanted to look nice because Grandma Rose always said if you look good, you feel good. I also wanted Vivi to be proud to be my friend. When we arrived at her office, it was not what I expected. There was no elevator or big huge windows like the lawyers' offices on TV. The office building was one story, and there were several desks with ladies typing. Vivi informed me that there was a receptionist who was the lady who greets customers, and answers the phone. There was also a secretary for each lawyer, and they all sat near each other. There was another lady there who was a research assistant/paralegal. I did not know what that was, but I acted like I did. There was a lobby with a couch, a few seats, and coffee tables with magazines for people to read while they waited. Then we were buzzed into another door that led to a hallway. As we walked down the hall, we passed the open doors of the lawyers' personal offices. Each partner had a big office, and the regular lawyers had smaller offices, each with a desk and two chairs. At the end of the hall there was a break room where the ladies made coffee, and there was a mini refrigerator where they had sodas and water. There were also snacks and a small table with two chairs. Around the corner from the break room there were two bathrooms, one for ladies and one for men. There was only one toilet in each bathroom, and the doors locked from the inside for privacy. Even though it did not look like what I had imagined, I was still excited to be there.

Vivi's office was at the end of the hall, next to the break room. She had a large desk, and her wall was decorated with beautiful artwork from Africa. She had her diploma on the small wall next to her desk, and it was in a huge frame that looked very fancy. She graduated from North Carolina State University and then attended UNC Chapel Hill for her law degree. If you're from North Carolina, you know how rare this is. Most people choose either one school or the other. Nobody goes to both schools! It's against the law here in Tobacco Road. She must be a very special person.

I spent the entire day with Vivi learning new things I never knew that black ladies could do. She went to a meeting with other lawyers and people from her office, and everyone there called her Miss Smalls or ma'am. She was a real boss lady, and nobody told her what to do. She also made several phone calls, and she sounded so confident and in charge. Not once did she ask how she looked or check to see if her hair was just right like Mommy did all of the time. Don't get me wrong, she was put together, but she did not keep looking at herself in the mirror. Vivi's hair was natural, and she wore it in an afro. I thought that was odd for a lawyer because the only people who went around with afros were the back to Africa types. They wore dashikis and always had their fist in the air. She was the business type who had employees, and met with white people all day. Vivi said she was proud of her African heritage. She was an educated sista; she wanted to show people that she could show her black pride, and still be successful. When we went to court, you could see the other lawyers and the judge respected her. She was forceful, and used all of these lawyer words. I had no idea what she was saying half of the time. She had given me a pad and paper to take notes when I was with her, and I wrote down the words that I thought she said. Later I would get out my dictionary to see what she was talking about. I never knew a woman could be so in charge, and still look so pretty. I always thought a woman could either be smart or pretty, but Vivi showed me you could be both. I looked up to her, but I also knew I did not want to be a lawyer. Most of her day was very boring, and I could not see myself doing that job. I wanted to be a writer.

That evening when we returned to her house, Vivi changed into a loose fitting dress, tied a beautiful scarf around her hair, and put on some flat slippers. She washed off the little bit of makeup she was wearing, and asked what I wanted for dinner. I thought I would treat her to a nice, home-cooked meal since she was working so hard at making me feel welcome. I volunteered to cook, but she wanted pizza. That was a treat for me because we never had pizza at home. Mommy said pizza would make her skin break out, and therefore it was off limits. I remember Daddy taking me to a pizza parlor once when we left church. I was not as careful as I should have been, and got some grease on my dress. Mommy was hopping mad when we got home, but it was worth it. That pizza was so good. I remembered it was called New York style, and it had pepperoni and cheese. I asked Vivi if we could have that kind, and she was down. We drank

Pepsi and ate pizza while we listened to her records. I had so much fun talking and laughing with Vivi. She was like the big sister I always wanted Queenie to be. I wondered why it couldn't be like this all of the time. If only my mommy and sister liked me we could be having fun like this together. I guess it was time for me to stop thinking about them because it was painfully obvious that I was not missed or loved by my family. How was it that a stranger could treat me so was well, and really like me after knowing me for a couple of days? Maybe this was a sign of things to come. Maybe, just maybe, the kids at school will start liking me, and I can have friends my own age. I'd find out in the morning because I could finally go back to school!

The next morning I woke up early, before the alarm clock had a chance to go off. I was nervous and excited like it was the first day of school. The funny thing was, the school year was almost over, and soon it would be time for summer break. I usually loved summertime because Daddy and I always took a vacation together. He always chose a new place every year, and I had a collection of post-cards and snow globes from every trip we took. He always said it was important to travel, and learn about other people's ways. This year there would be no trip, so I had to think of something else to do. In the meantime, I still had to finish the school year. I got up, took a shower, and dressed. Then I made tea and toast for Vivi. She rarely ate a large breakfast she told me yesterday. She liked to have toast with butter & jam and hot tea that was flavored with sugar & cream. I had never seen anyone drink cream in their tea, but Vivi insisted that there was a whole country of people who do it. She had visited London, England, and that is where she learned how to drink proper tea. I still thought drinking hot tea with cream was weird, but I was a child, what did I know? If Vivi liked it, maybe I would too.

Vivi drove me to school in her sporty Mercedes, and said she would pick me up around 2:30pm. I waved to her as she drove away and then panic set in. What if Nicole and her friends decided to start some mess? I knew Mr. George would not tolerate me fighting again, and I did not want to get in any trouble while I was staying with Vivi. What she thought of me was very important, and I did not want her to think I was unruly. I would be the sweet little girl that Daddy and Grandma Rose taught me to be. If something went down, I would just walk away. I walked into my classroom, and it was as if I was never gone. Everyone was in their little cliques, and Mrs. Myers was sitting at her desk getting things ready for us. She looked up when I walked in and smiled. "Hi, Zora," she said. "I am happy you are back with us. I hope you got all of the aggression out, and are ready to get along with everyone." "Yes ma'am," I replied. Mrs. Myers just kept on talking, "I was out for a few days with a cold so the class had a substitute teacher. There wasn't any homework, so you did not miss many assignments. You can stay in during recess to catch up on what you missed," she informed me. I did not have a choice, and I think she was trying to avoid any confrontations on my first day back. She knew Nicole hadn't forgotten what I did to her, and she did not want me to get in trouble all over again. I took my seat and waited for the bell to ring.

My first day back was good. I did not have a care in the world until a man came to the door and asked Mrs. Myers if he could speak with me. I was told to follow the man to the office, and then into a room. I did not want to be alone with a strange man, and I began to cry. What was he going to do to me? I begged Mrs. Myers to call Vivi, and she did. I held onto the column that stood in the middle of the office. and refused to go into that room with that man. Did Mr. Samuels tell him how good I was at giving head? Did he want to find out for himself? Maybe he was here to make me do other things that I did not want to do. I thought all of this was over, and I just could not allow him to touch me. Mr. George tried talking to me, but he only made it worse. Was he in on it too? What did he want me to do to him? I refused to be used and passed around like those ladies on the street. I wanted to be somebody, and I wasn't going to be the girl that all the men abused. I was feeling myself start to go crazy when in walked Vivi. As soon as I saw her I rushed to her and told her that

45

that man was going to hurt me, and I was afraid. I was screaming and crying, and I did not know if she understood me. She took one look around the office, and then in a calm, low voice said, "Zora, I need you to calm down so I can help you. Nobody is going to hurt you, I promise." I stopped crying, and began to calm down. "Now, somebody tell me what is going on here," Vivi demanded. The man in the suit walked up, and I hid behind Vivi. "My name is Detective Johnson, and I need to speak with this child about an ongoing investigation. I asked her to come into the room with me, and she freaked out," he explained. "Well, Detective Johnson, if you know Zora's case, you can understand why it might be scary for a little girl to be alone with a strange man in a closed room. What were you thinking? She's been through too much, and I refuse to allow her to be harmed anymore. You should have at least called me before coming so I could warn her." Vivi was getting angry, and her voice began to shake. "I meant no harm, ma'am. I just need to inform her of the outcome of her case, and I didn't think she would react that way to a cop," the detective said. "Did you tell her who you were, or did you just come get her, and attempt to take her in the room? You should really be more aware of children's feelings, and what can happen when they have been traumatized."

After I settled down, Vivi, the detective, and I went into the room to talk. He informed us that Mr. Samuels was released from custody. He said there was not enough evidence to prosecute him, and someone called a DA, decided to cut him loose. Since there were no witnesses and no medical evidence they could not hold him. The detective said he believed me, but the law would not allow for punishment. Vivi was upset, but she informed me that sometimes these things happened. She reassured me that I would not have to go back and live with my mommy because she had been to family court this morning, and the judge awarded custody to my uncle and his wife. They lived in California, but were going to move back to North Carolina because of my circumstances. I remembered meeting them when I was 7 years old. Uncle Jim was my daddy's younger brother, and they looked a lot alike. He married a very pretty lady named Terri, and she was very nice. I remember her giving me a bottle of perfume, and telling me that I was cute. She made me feel very special, and I never forgot that.

Apparently my mommy did not put up a fight in court. In fact she was happy to sign over her parental rights, according to Vivi. I knew Mommy hated me, but I thought she would at least have some love for me deep down. I guess she chose Mr. Samuels over me, and if that meant I did not ever have to see his face again then I would pay the price of losing my mommy. Would I ever see her again? If I did see her, would she hug me or hit me? What would I tell people? I was sad and confused that Mommy did not want me, but I could not let that ruin my life. Daddy taught me that. He loved, me and he made sure I still felt his love even after he was gone. Grandma Rose loved me, too. She always said that God would protect me and that I was special. Grandma Rose was right about one thing, when I asked, for help God sent me Vivi. I will say a prayer every night from now on to thank God for his gift. I would have to live off of the love Daddy and Grandma Rose gave me until I could find someone else who loved me.

Chapter 8: Uncle Jim and Aunt Terri

Vivi explained that Uncle Jim and Aunt Terri really wanted me. Aunt Terri was unable to have babies, and she really wanted a child. They said I was a blessing from God. Uncle Jim was excited to be moving back to North Carolina and taking over my daddy's business. Daddy had put him in charge of his company until I was old enough to run it. I didn't even know what they did at the company. I would ask Uncle Jim when he got here. Vivi said they would be arriving in about two weeks. They needed time to pack, and then travel here across country. I was excited to see them and wished I could be in the car when they were driving. I longed to see California and all of the other states in between there and North Carolina.

In the meantime I would stay with Vivi, and we would continue our slumber party every night. I liked staying with her, and she always let me choose what we had for dinner. We had so much fun hanging out together. We made plans to go on a road trip to Carowinds for the weekend. I had never been to an amusement park before, and I was super excited. Daddy had planned to take me to Disney World in Florida this summer, but of course that was out now. Friday afternoon I was super excited. When Vivi picked me up from school, I had a ton of questions. "How long does it take to drive to Charlotte? Will we need to stop for gas? What will we eat for dinner?

Where will we spend the night? Can we really stay all day long on Saturday? Did they have roller-coasters, and am I big enough to ride them?" I wore poor Vivi out with my curiosity. Vivi said, "It takes about 6 hours to drive to Charlotte; yes, we will stop for gas; we can go to McDonald's for dinner; we are staying at the Holiday Inn, and yes, I was big enough to ride the many roller-coasters that they have." She chuckled as she answered me, and I think she was just as excited as I was.

When we finally arrived at the front gate of Carowinds, I was amazed. It was bigger than I imagined. There were people dressed as cartoon characters that welcomed us into the park, and then there were games to play, a huge food court, and roller-coasters! I was so excited to ride my very first rollercoaster that I forgot I was afraid of heights. It never dawned on me that I would be high off of the ground, and in a little box that had little to no protection. We stood in line forever, and finally when it was our chance to ride, fear set in. I got into the box, and the operator pulled down the safety harness. I could see all of the other kids with smiles on their faces, but my stomach started to hurt. As the coaster started moving to exit the safety of the depot, I panicked. The coaster rounded the corner, and all I could see was daylight and how much space there was between the track and the ground. The highest I had been off the ground was in my willow tree in the back yard. I was instantly frozen with fear, and wanted to get off. It was too late, the coaster started moving faster and faster, and I wanted to cry. I decided to close my eyes because the fact that I may fall to my death seemed less real.

When the ride was over, I was shaking and felt sick. I never wanted to feel like that again, so when Vivi asked if I wanted to ride another roller-coaster, I shouted, "NO!" She laughed and asked what was wrong. "I just didn't like it. I thought I would love it, but it made me not want to leave the ground ever again," I whined. Vivi laughed and laughed. "I am happy to hear you say that. I didn't want to say anything, but I was scared out of my skin," Vivi confessed. We decided that the rest of the day should be spent winning stuffed animals and eating. We had such a good time all weekend. It was the most fun I remember having besides when Daddy took me on our summer trips. I would treasure this weekend forever because I spent it with my first real friend.

Two weeks passed so quickly, and I was surprised to hear that my mommy and the rest of the family had moved out of my house. I was excited to see my uncle and aunt again, but I was a little scared at the same time. Would they like me? Would Uncle Jim be like Daddy, or would he be like Mr. Samuels? Would Aunt Terri be like Mommy, or would she be like Vivi? Vivi told me that everything would be alright, and as soon as school was out, I would get to start my new life. She also said for me not to worry. She had met my uncle and aunt, and they were very nice people. "Zora, you know I will always be here for you, right? Just because Jim and Terri are your guardians doesn't mean we have to stop being friends. We can still hang out and have fun together."

After school Vivi picked me up as usual, but this time she drove me to my house instead of hers. She explained that all of my stuff was still in my room, and that Uncle Jim and Aunt Terri had been moving all day. As soon as we pulled up outside, I knew that something was different. I could feel love coming from underneath the door. Then the door flung open, and I was looking at my daddy. I couldn't believe my eyes. I began crying and immediately rushed into his arms. I just couldn't help myself; he looked so much like Daddy that I thought it was him for a brief second. Uncle Jim was taken aback and didn't know what to do. He just held me and let me get my tears out. After I calmed down, I apologized and explained why I acted so crazy. "I'm sorry, Uncle Jim. It's just that you look just like Daddy, and I miss him so much," I cried. "It's ok, baby girl. You must have thought you were seeing a ghost. Barry and I always looked more like twins than just brothers. Zora, you remember your Aunt Terri." I released my kung fu grip, and reached out to shake hands with Aunt

Terri. She laughed and said, "Don't come over here with that hand-shake. I'm a hugger!" She hugged me tightly, and it felt good. I was happy they were here. Maybe now I could have a real family. I wish Daddy and Grandma Rose were here with us. We could be one big, happy family.

Vivi helped me bring my bags in, and then she said her goodbyes. She made me promise to call her the next day to let her know how everything was going. I hugged her, and thanked her for everything she had done for me. I promised to call, and then she left. I was no longer nervous, and I felt like I was in good hands. After all, Uncle Jim was Daddy's little brother, and they were raised in the same home by Grandma Rose. I was sure he was a good person. Aunt Terri must be pretty cool also because he married her. I decided that since they had been moving all day I should cook for them, but Aunt Terri said she wanted to go out to eat. They freshened up, and we went to a local restaurant for dinner. I am usually shy around strangers, but I found it easy to talk to my uncle and aunt. Uncle Jim kept calling me Babygirl, and Aunt Terri nicknamed me Butterfly. I liked having nick-names because it made me feel important to someone. Nobody ever gives a person a nickname unless they care about them.

My uncle and aunt sure had different taste in decorating than Mommy. Their furniture was normal, but they had all of this black artwork that they hung on the walls. Aunt Terri was big into art, and she took pride in her collection. They loved animal print, and even had a rug made from a real tiger! It still had the head on it and everything. I had read about bear skin rugs, but never tiger. They had traveled to Africa and brought back wood carvings and lots of African print material. Aunt Terri sewed, and she was able to make slip-covers for the furniture. It looked like something from National Geographic. I wasn't sure if I liked their style, but I was happy they were there.

Aunt Terri wore her hair natural, and always had a scarf tied around it. She used African prints and bright colors to match her outfits. Nobody in the neighborhood had clothes like her, and she stood out. She was a very beautiful woman with silky chocolate skin and curly hair. She was a bit on the chubby side, but Uncle Jim seemed to like it. He was always pinching her on her bottom or rubbing on her big thighs. I thought she could be a movie star if she wanted. She smelled like sweet flowers, and was always in a good mood. She had a big beautiful smile and loved to be hugged. I liked her very much.

We all settled into the house quickly, and it became more of a home to me than in all the time I lived there with Mommy. Before I knew it, the school year was coming to an end, and it was time to think about what I would do with myself for the summer. Vivi and I were still best of friends, and she asked if I could spend a week with her during the summer. There was some sort of summer camp her law office was sponsoring, and she wanted me to attend. Uncle Jim and Aunt Terri agreed to let me go as long as I called to check in daily. They really liked having me around, and I liked being there. Things were getting back to normal. I still missed Daddy and Grandma Rose, but I had Uncle Jim to remind me of their love. He said God sent him to shower me with the love Daddy would have given me if he was still alive. I had always been a daddy's girl, and now his brother was here for me to love. Maybe, just maybe I will be ok.

Chapter 9: She's Back

On the last day of school, I was so excited that I never saw her standing there. I was rushing to get home when she called my name. "Zora," she called out to me. I froze in my tracks. I had not heard that voice in a few weeks, and it made my blood run cold. "Zora, I know you hear me. Come here." I did not turn around because I was afraid I would turn to stone. "Girl, you are still my child, and I raised you to do as I say," Mommy called out to me. I took off running. I did not know what she wanted, but I no longer felt the need to do as I was told. She never loved me, and now she was coming to ruin my summer. I ran so fast I almost fell into the front door.

"Zora, what's wrong?" asked Aunt Terri as soon as she saw my face. "My mommy was at the school, and she was after me," I answered. "What do you mean she was after you?" Aunt Terri replied with caution. Before I could answer her someone was turning the doorknob. It was her! She walked right in like she still owned the place. Aunt Terri turned into a grizzly bear protecting her young. "Stop right there. You can't just walk up in here. In case you missed the memo, you don't live here anymore!" Aunt Terri did not play. As she was talking, she was picking up a large wooden cane that was on display next to the chair. "You can just turn yourself around and leave," she continued. Mommy was never one to back down from a challenge, but you could tell she was scared.

"This is my house, and that is my daughter, and I will stay as long as I want. What are you going to do about it, Terri?" Mommy taunted. Aunt Terri began to walk toward Mommy when out of nowhere Uncle Jim appeared. "Teresa, how nice to see you; did you come to visit Zora?" he said cheerfully. Uncle Jim hated to see my Aunt Terri upset, and he tried his best to stop the fight before it started. "No, I didn't come for a visit Jim. I am here to tell y'all to get the hell out of my house, and leave my child when you do," Mommy snarled. "Look, bitch, I told you to get out. I won't say it again. The next thing you are gonna hear is this cane going upside your head," Aunt Terri chimed. Mommy knew Aunt Terri meant what she said. She had this look on her face that I had never seen before. "If you come back around here I will personally kick your ass to China and back. You hear me? If you think I'm playin', try me!"

Mommy turned to leave, and then she looked back at me and said, "You are my flesh and blood. You think Terri has saved you from my wrath, but I will find you when you least expect it. I'm gonna kill you for ruining my life." I got goose bumps, but I did not let her see that I was afraid. I walked right up to her and said, "That little girl you used to beat is no longer here. I am not afraid of you anymore. If you try to hurt me, I will fight back, and it won't be pretty. You are my mother, and I love you, but I will not allow you to kill me. You no longer have power over me!" With those words, I blew her a kiss and walked away.

Tears flowed down my face as I walked away from Mommy. How could she think that I ruined her life when it was the other way around? She hated me since before I was born, and I had done nothing but exist. I was an obedient daughter, and I loved her truly. She showed me no love, and killed my daddy with her selfishness. She allowed her boyfriend to rape my mouth, and that ended up killing my grandma. Mommy deserved every bad thing that was happening to her, and I still felt bad about it. Even now, I wanted her to have a nice life, but she was out for revenge for something she thought I did. Why couldn't she face the reality that I was just a little girl who needed and wanted to be loved by her mother? I made up my mind then and there I would no longer need or want her in my life. She was not willing to love me, so I pushed a button inside myself and turned my love for her off. If she came after me, I swore to myself that I would only hurt her, but not kill her. Maybe one day I would be able to turn that button back on, but until then, I could no longer think of her as my mommy. Teresa Langston was now my arch enemy. I would continue to pray for her, but I would be watching my back.

Uncle Jim hated to see me cry, and he put his arm around my shoulders and held me close. I emptied my tears onto his shirt, and when I was finished he and Aunt Terri wiped my face. They told me that my mom would never hurt me again. They would always be there to protect me. They told me how much they loved me, and tried to reassure me that I was safe. Just then I remembered that it was officially summer vacation, and I refused to cry one more second.

"Aunt Terri and Uncle Jim, I don't want to be unhappy tonight. Let's celebrate the last day of school!" I said out of nowhere. They both laughed, and agreed that we should have a three person party. Aunt Terri and I cooked dinner, and baked cupcakes for dessert. While we were cooking, Uncle Jim decorated the living room with streamers and balloons. We had hot dogs and french fries for dinner, and as a special treat we ate in the living room. While we ate, Uncle Jim played some of his records. He and Aunt Terri showed me some of their dance moves after we ate. They were so funny twisting and turning around in the living room. You could see how much they loved each other, and it was great to be in a happy home. When I went to bed that night, I dreamed of dancing and cupcakes and laughing.

The next morning I got to sleep in. Aunt Terri did not start her job until after the summer break so we could spend some time hanging out together. She would be working all the way in Raleigh, which was about an hour away. She taught African American studies in California and would be doing the same at North Carolina State University. She was a very smart lady and encouraged me to read more African American literature. She absolutely loved that I had a passion for reading, and had a small book collection of my own. Daddy had given me books of poetry by Langston Hughes and Edgar Allan Poe because he always liked them. I did not understand most of the poems, but I liked the way they rolled off of my tongue when I read them out loud. Aunt Terri decided not to teach summer school so we could have some bonding time. I was happy that she cared enough to do that. This was going to be a big summer for me. I would be turning 10 in July, and I was going to go to Vacation Bible School at the church where Daddy and I were members. I also wanted to join the Summer Reading Program at the Public Library. I read about it on the board at school, and I was looking forward to reading about all the new adventures I would have in all the new books.

When I came downstairs, Aunt Terri was sitting at the kitchen table reading the paper and drinking some hot tea. She had a box of cereal on the table waiting for me, and I couldn't believe my eyes. It was Captain Crunch! That was my favorite, and I was so greedy that I ate two bowls. Aunt Terri was happy that I liked her surprised, and then she said, "Zora, we need to talk about what happened yesterday." I was taken aback, but Aunt Terri kept going, "I feel bad that you saw me acting out of character, and I did not mean to disrespect your mom." I stopped her there, "Aunt Terri, I don't have a mom; I never have. My daddy and Grandma Rose were the only people who ever showed me love until you and Uncle Jim came to take care of me. I am fine with that. My brother and sister never really liked me, and my own mother hated me my entire life. I survived because God loved me enough to send you here. I don't really need my mom in my life because she was so mean to me. I guess I would miss her if she ever showed me just a little tiny bit of love, but she never has." Aunt Terri was sitting at the table listening to me, and the more I talked, the more she cried. I did not want to upset her, so I stopped talking. "Zora, I am sorry that you have never known a mother's love, but I will do my best to show you how much Auntie cares for you." She hugged me, and held me very tight. I loved Aunt Terri, and was happy she loved me, too.

Later that day, Aunt Terri took me to the library to sign up for the Summer Reading Program. The librarian said I could start the next day. She provided a list of books, and informed me that I should read as many as I could for the next couple of weeks. There would be a ceremony on the last day, and there would be a prize for the person who read the most books. I wanted that prize, and nobody was going to beat me out. The next day I couldn't wait to get to the library. Aunt Terri dropped me off at 10 am and said she would be back at noon. I whined and begged her to let me stay until at least 2:00pm. That way I would be able to read more books, and get a jump start on my prize. She was happy to let me stay longer because she said I was using my time wisely. Inside the library, the lady in charge of the reading program welcomed us all. There were about 10 kids all together and I was excited to meet them. I did not know there were other kids that liked to read like I did. We had to go to the shelves, pull the book we wanted, and then we would sit somewhere on the children's side to read. Once we were finished, we would return the book to the desk, and the librarian would mark that book read on her list. She would keep track of all of the books that we read until the final day. We were given a name tag, and sent off to our adventures. I must have read about five books before I felt a tap on my shoulder; it was Aunt Terri coming to get me. I was surprised to see her because I was lost in my book. I was almost finished and asked Aunt Terri if she wouldn't mind waiting until I was done. She agreed and decided to go browse in the adult section. She told me she would return in 10 minutes, and that was enough time. I was off to a good start, and looked forward to the rest of the week.

On the third day of the program, Aunt Terri had some errands to run and asked if I would be alright walking home alone. I was a big girl and had walked home before, so I told her yes. On the way out of the library I heard that voice again. She was back, and this time she sounded and looked drunk. "Zora, you little nerd, I knew I would find you here. I've been watching you for the last couple of days, and waiting to catch you alone," Teresa Langston called out to me. I didn't want to show any weakness, so I approached her, and looked her right in the eye. "What do you want from me?" I asked. "You obviously hate me so why do you keep coming around? If it's money you want, I don't have any. You will have to go see my lawyer." That enraged her. "You little bitch, you listen to me. I'm still your mom, and you are going to show me some respect. I hate you, huh? You are so right! I have always hated you!" she yelled. "What do I want? I want you to leave my man alone. That's what I want. All he talks about is you, and how you are so much better than me at giving head. I want you to stay away from him or I'm going to kick your little ass," she continued. "How can you stand here and say that to me? Your man? I don't want your so called man. He raped my mouth, and I did not like it. You must be crazy!" I yelled. She drew back to hit me, and I pushed her down on the ground. "Leave me alone, you drunk! I don't ever want to see you again. Stop coming around me because you are dead to me." I left her lying on the ground, and walked home. I was surprised that I wasn't scared. She was dead to me, and now she knew it!

Chapter 10: Summer Time and the Living is... Easy?

I decided not to tell Aunt Terri about my encounter with Teresa Langston. I did not want Aunt Terri to get in any trouble, because I knew she would lose it. I pretended it never happened and, concentrated on the good things that were happening. I enjoyed the remaining week at the library reading all kinds of books that I never heard of. I was taken to Arabia to hobnob with princes and princesses; I went to New York City and learned about city children; I even went Europe and played with orphans. There were so many adventures I did not know what to do with myself. On the last day, I was sad to leave. We had the ceremony as promised, and I won the top prize for the most books read. Aunt Terri was so proud of me she stood up, and clapped as I went to the front to accept my award. I was given a journal, a fancy pen, and a ribbon to signify that I was the best reader. I had never been the best at anything before, and it felt great. The lady said I should use the journal to write my own stories. I was so excited because I always wanted to write my own stories; I just never knew that it was possible until now. After reading all of those books, my imagination was working overtime, and I was eager to start writing. I knew I wouldn't be able to write stories like the ones I read, but if I could write something good maybe, just maybe it could change someone's life.

Now that the Summer Reading Program was over, I would be

starting Vacation Bible School on Monday. I always enjoyed going to VBS - that's what everybody called it. I got to see all of the ladies from church, and they were always very nice to me. Whenever Daddy and I went to church those same ladies always made a point to hug me, fuss over me, and give me cake. I didn't know who made the cakes at church, but they were the best, especially the ones with that white icing. There was a church van that would pick me up, and drop me off down the street from the house. VBS lasted a few hours every day, and that would give me plenty of time to spend with Aunt Terri.

VBS was very different from Sunday school. It was way more fun, and we got to do arts and crafts, sing songs, and play outside. It only lasted one week, and on Friday we usually had a play for our parents. Since Aunt Terri was off from work, she promised to come to our play because Daddy couldn't be there this year. We normally sang songs, and dressed up in costumes. Last year our teacher helped us make our own costumes, and we practiced the song over and over so that we would be good. We had so much fun, and Daddy said I did a good job in the play. I knew I couldn't sing very well, so I just moved my mouth during the song. I knew all the words, but it sounded horrible when I sang to myself in my room. No one would tell me because they did not want to hurt my feelings, but I knew I would never make a living as a singer.

This year, on the first day of VBS, we studied about Jesus and his disciples. We also learned about unconditional love. I liked the way our teachers took God's love, and applied it to our lives. The only problem was everyone had to give an example of unconditional love. As they went around the room, each child talked about their mom. I was a little sad and panicked, because I did not know who I could use as an example. At the last moment I blurted out, "My daddy was the best example of unconditional love I ever knew."

I don't know what came over me, but as soon as I said it I burst into tears and couldn't stop crying. All of the kids looked at me like I was crazy until the teacher explained that my daddy had recently passed away. The other kids seemed to understand and left me alone. I did not want this to be a sad day, but something just came over me. I was able to pull myself together, and make it through the first day. I was sure the next day would be better. One of the teachers pulled me to the side after class, and asked if I was alright. She also told me she understood the loss I was feeling, and that anytime I felt overwhelmed it was ok to cry. She suggested that I make a point to talk to God every night before I go to sleep, and ask him to help me with my pain. "Just give it to God," she said. I thanked her for the advice, but it felt weird talking to her about my personal business. "Yes, ma'am., thank you, but I don't want to miss my ride," I said before she could ask me any personal questions. I was relieved when she let me go.

Most of the kids rode the van home, but on the way to drop off the last few kids there was a problem with the engine, and the van broke down. Since those of us that were left lived two miles or less away we told the driver we would walk the rest of the way. He was fine with that since we were walking in a group. He made us promise to stay together, and look out for each other. I took my back pack and started walking with a boy named Marvin. He was nice to me at church, and he lived a few streets over from me. Two other kids decided to walk with us, but they were older than me, and I didn't know their names. The two older kids started picking on me for crying during VBS.

"You're such a cry baby!" the one girl in the yellow said. "I can't believe how much of a baby you are. Especially since you are the tallest one in the class," the girl in red put her two cents in. "I thought for sure her mama was gonna have to come get her," the girl in yellow continued. "That ho ain't got no mama," the girl in red chimed in. They started laughing, but I could see Marvin was embarrassed for me. He did not say anything, but he did not laugh either. The girls took turns saying more and more mean things and eventually started pushing me back and forth to each other like a pin ball machine. I did not want to get into a fight because I don't like hurting people. I had so much rage built up in me that I could really do those girls harm, so I decided to run ahead, and take a short cut through the park. I remember my daddy telling me not to walk in the park alone, but I had no choice. Besides, we always came to the park for school outings, and on the weekends for picnics. I never saw any danger when we were there, so I figured it would be ok this one time.

As soon as I passed the train that all the little kids rode when they came to the park, I got a strange feeling. The hair stood up on the back of my neck, and I got scared. I looked around but I did not see anyone. Straight ahead was a huge oak tree that had been there for hundreds of years. There was a story going around that Civil War soldiers hung and tortured slaves from that tree. The slaves supposedly haunted the park, and their spirits lived in that tree. It was spooky not because it was early in the afternoon, but because the tree was so large it had a huge shadow, and the whole area around it was dark. I decided to take my chances with the ghosts rather than to go back to the street and run into those mean girls. I told myself that if I ran, it would be quick and easy to get past the tree. I was scared, and I felt panic set in. As I passed the big oak tree, I felt a hand grab me. Because I was running, I jolted backwards and almost fell to the ground. I turned to see who had a hold of me, and came face to face with my nightmare. Instead of the ghost of a dead slave there he was the boogie man himself. Mr. Samuels was standing there grinning at me and laughing. "Hey little bitch, did you think you got rid of me?" he snarled. I screamed, and he slapped me over and over. I just knew he was going to really hurt me now, because nobody was here to save me. I wanted to cry, but I decided that I would not give him the satisfaction. He wanted me to be scared, so I acted like I wasn't. I began saying the Lord's Prayer out loud, and it made him angry.

"The Lord is my shepherd, I shall not want. He maketh me to lie down in green pastures. He leadeth me beside the still waters…"

Mr. Samuels told me to shut up, but I kept saying the prayer. "He restoreth my soul. He leadeth me in the path of righteousness for his name's sake. Yea, though I walk through the valley and the shadows of death... *I WILL FEAR NO EVIL!*' Just then something came over me, and all I wanted to do was fight. I would not allow him to hurt me again. He had a knife and threatened me, "If you don't stop that crazy church shit, I'm going to slit your throat." I kept right on reciting the prayer.

"For thou art with me..." I continued, and I started fighting as hard as I could. I smacked and clawed him in the face. When that did not work, I bit his arm. That was a big mistake because he punched me in the head. It felt like he bashed me with a steel pipe. I continued to fight him, but I wasn't strong enough, and he threw me to the ground.

"I'm gonna get your ass now. I don't care how old you are. This time I'm fuckin' you," he hissed through his teeth. I looked around for a stick or a rock or something, but there wasn't one. "Get off of me," I yelled. He was on top of me, and he was very heavy. I tried to roll from underneath, but I was pinned. I thought I was going to throw up because his breath smelled like old whiskey, and his body reeked of funk like he hadn't washed in a few days.

"I said get off of me," I yelled again. When that did not work, I decided to keep praying, "Thy rod and thy staff they comfort me. Thou preparest a table before me in the presence of mine enemies..."

"Shut that racket up. I can't think with that church talk buzzin' in my ear," he demanded. He pulled up my dress, and ripped off my panties. I tried to kick him, but he laid on one of my legs, and pushed the other open with his thigh. He was on top of me, and pushed his thing in me. I screamed, "Don't do that," but he didn't care. He began pushing his hips back and forth very fast. It hurt so bad that as I screamed I thought I was listening to someone else. It felt as if I left my body, and whatever Mr. Samuels was doing was no longer happening to me. I must have passed out from the pain because when I came to, he was looking at me all crazy. "Bitch, I thought I killed you. Don't you do that again. You better stay awake." I don't know what he did to me when I passed out, but I was sure I would not be able to walk.

"Get off of me," I started yelling again. I saw blood spilling out onto the grass, and I knew it was mine. I thought I was going to die, and I panicked. This time I did not care if he knew I was afraid. I was screaming at the top of my lungs for help. Then out of nowhere I heard someone say, "Dad, get off of her!" It was Big Willie, and he was mad. Willie took a rock and pounded Mr. Samuels in his back until he was no longer on top of me.

"That's my sister; how could you do that to her?" he continued. Willie jumped on top of Mr. Samuels and yelled for me to run. "Zora, get out of here. Run!" I tried to get on my feet, but I was in too much pain, and my legs would not work. When I looked down, and saw all that blood everywhere I got queasy. I did not know what to do, so I started crawling away all the while screaming for help. "Somebody please help us!" I kept crawling until I reached the street. Finally a policeman came around the corner. I guess he heard me screaming and came to help. It was him, the same officer that came to my house to report that Grandma Rose died. "Zora, what's going on?" he said with fear in his voice. He must have seen the blood and was afraid. "Mr. Samuels just attacked me under the oak tree, and now my brother is fighting him off," I screamed. "He's got a knife," I warned.

Mr. Samuels broke away from Big Willie, and ran when he saw the officer coming. The officer did not want to leave us alone, so Mr. Samuels got away. He called an ambulance to take me to the hospital, but I refused to go without Big Willie. He was hurt too, and we couldn't just leave him there. The police officer rode with us, and he talked to me to try and calm me down. I did not want anyone to see my private parts, and I did not want the man in the ambulance to touch me. I felt dirty, and all I wanted to do was take a bath and go to sleep. I did not want to think about what happened and definitely did not want to talk about it.

Aunt Terri and Uncle Jim were waiting at the hospital when we arrived. The police had called to tell them what happened, and they rushed right over. Aunt Terri was crying and wanted to hold me but the doctors would not let her. Uncle Jim had to carry her out of the room so the doctors could treat me. There was a man doctor and a woman doctor, but I did not want either of them to look at me. I was in a lot of pain, and I was still bleeding, but I did not care. I just wanted to be left alone. They gave me some kind of drug and said it would help me to calm down; all it did was make me loopy. I felt like I was looking at everyone through a cloudy window. I started yelling because the man doctor tried to look under the sheet at my pocketbook. I think I kicked him in the face because he started cursing, and told the nurses to hold me down. Aunt Terri burst into the room to see what was going on, and the man doctor told her to leave. "Ma'am, you can't be in here. You need to leave," he instructed

"I'm not leaving her in here with you. Can't you see she is afraid of men! Are you sure you're a doctor because you act like a damn fool!" Aunt Terri screamed. "If anyone is going to look at her private parts it should be a female! Didn't they teach you how to deal with rape victims in medical school?" They started arguing back and forth until the lady doctor spoke up, and said she should be the one to do the examination. She made the man doctor leave the room. Aunt Terri held my hand while the doctor did her job. At first she was very gentle, but then it started to feel like she was pulling something out of me. It hurt so badly, and I wanted her to stop. "Aunt Terri please make her stop," I begged. "Butterfly, this is only going to take a few more minutes, and I need you to be brave" Aunt Terri said. The doctor finished poking around my pocketbook and asked Aunt Terri if she could speak with her and Uncle Jim in private. That made me worry because adults only have private talks when something is wrong. Besides, my pocketbook hurt even worse after she was down there. I started to cry because I was hurting, and I was scared. I wanted my daddy.

When Aunt Terri and the lady doctor came back in they explained that my injuries were worse than they thought, and I would need surgery. My mind blanked out, and I did not know what to do. I started crying harder and screaming for my daddy. The nurse asked Uncle Jim to come in the room because she thought he was my daddy. Since he was the closest thing I had to a father now, I clung to Uncle Jim and begged, "Please don't let them operate on me. I'm afraid that I will die." Uncle Jim calmed me down by singing *I Heard It Through the Grapevine* by Marvin Gaye.

That was his favorite song, and he always made me laugh when he sung because he did a silly dance with it. I tried to sing backup for him, and he always made a joke about my singing. This time he said, "Maybe the doctor can add some singing juice to your voice while you're in there, and then you'll be ready to sing with a big dog like me." We both laughed, and he hugged me tight. I agreed to have the surgery because Aunt Terri and Uncle Jim said it would be the right thing to do. "Don't worry, Babygirl, I will never let anything else happen to you, I promise," Uncle Jim whispered in my ear as the doctor wheeled me into surgery. I felt sure that he meant it because he had tears in his eyes.

Chapter 11: The Road to Recovery

When I woke up I was groggy, but I could see several faces in the room. Of course Aunt Terri and Uncle Jim were there, and now so was Vivi, Big Willie, and the policeman. I heard the officer say Mr. Samuels was captured in the park. He had fallen asleep in one of the gazebos, and they arrested him. Everyone seemed happy to hear the news, but still looked so sad; I knew it was because of me. I had to show them that I was alright. Nothing Mr. Samuels had done to me was going to keep me down. For the first time since Daddy and Grandma Rose died, I had people who loved me, and I was not going to let Mr. Samuels ruin that again.

"There she is," chimed Uncle Jim. "How are you feeling, Babygirl?" he asked. Before I could answer, Aunt Terri and Vivi darted over to the bed, and started fussing over me. "Do you need anything, Butterfly?" Aunt Terri asked. "Zora, are you in much pain?" Vivi added. I did not have a chance to answer because the doctor came in, and asked them to let me breathe. "Ladies please, stop fussing over the poor girl and let her rest." The doctor pulled back the sheet and examined my belly. It was sore, and there were stitches. Since nobody ever told me what kind of surgery I had, I had no idea that I was going to have stitches. "Doctor, will I have a big scar on my belly?" I asked. "Zora you will have a scar, but it will only be a small one," the doctor answered. "She seems to be doing well, and should be able to go home in a few days," the doctor told my family. My family… I liked thinking of them all as my family.

"Doctor, what exactly is wrong with me?" I asked. The entire room went silent, and nobody would look at me, not even Vivi. I got scared and began to panic. "What is it? Tell me, am I going to die?" Aunt Terri burst into tears, and I thought I was a goner for sure. I started crying, and started to think of all of the things that could be wrong with me. Did I have a heart condition? Did Mr. Samuels give me cancer? Did I need more operations? Nobody was saying anything, and I wanted to know. "Please tell me what's wrong. I need to know, even if it's cancer," I pleaded.

I guess it clicked in Aunt Terri's mind that if she didn't tell me, I would continue to make up illnesses, and worry myself to death. "Zora, what that bad man did to you caused a great deal of damage to your insides. The parts you need to have babies were very badly damaged, and you will not be able to have children when you grow up," Aunt Terri explained with tears streaming down her face. "Do you understand what I am telling you, Butterfly? You will never be a mommy." I saw how sad that made Aunt Terri, and everyone else in the room, but I did not share their sadness. I did not want to have kids anyway. I was too afraid I would grow up to be a bad mom just like mine. I would never want to do that to a child. Plus they are loud, and they stink. I could never tell them how I really felt about kids so I said, "Don't cry Aunt Terri, I will be ok. My mommy has 3 children and hates me, and you can't have babies, but you take great care of me. So I guess you don't have to actually have the baby to be a real mommy. You just have to show them love." I meant what I said to Aunt Terri because she does take great care of me, and she loves me more than my own mom. Aunt Terri grabbed me and hugged the stuffing out of me. "I love you, Butterfly, and don't you ever forget it," she exclaimed.

Just then I saw Big Willie sitting in the corner of the room looking very sad. He refused to look me in the eye, and seemed very upset. I asked Aunt Terri if I could speak to him in private, and she agreed. "Big Willie I just wanted to say thank you for saving me," I said in a low whisper. Did you hear me?" I asked. "Why are you thanking me? It was my dad who hurt you. Zora, I always liked you, and I felt really bad when your dad passed away. I never really talked to you that much, but I liked having you as a little sister. You were always a cool kid, and I couldn't figure out why you would lie on my dad. I never believed you when you said he was hurting you, and now look what he's done. I could have stopped him if I had believed you. One day I heard him and mom arguing about you, and he admitted to making you do those things. Then the day he attacked you, he got drunk and was bragging about going to hurt you again. I followed him when he left the house, but he lost me in the park. By the time I caught up to him, he was already hurting you. I am so sorry I couldn't stop him." Big Willie poured out his heart to me. He had never talked to me this much in our whole lives. I could tell he had been crying, and he felt like it was his fault that Mr. Samuels hurt me. "It wasn't your fault. If you would have said that about my daddy, I would never have believed you. I am just grateful that you were there to help," I replied.

"You were the only one in the house who was nice to me after my daddy died. Nobody even looked at me. At least you told me you were sorry, and that you liked my daddy. I have always looked up to you, and I liked it when you let me tag along sometimes when you go to play basketball. Please don't feel bad that you couldn't keep him from hurting me. At least you saved me like a big brother should. Thank you so much," I said as I held out my arms to give him a big hug. He let me hug him for a few seconds, and then he said he had to go because Mommy would be looking for him. He stood up, looked down at the floor and said quietly, "I love you Zora," and just like the wind, he was gone.

After Big Willie left, I started thinking about the future. Maybe he and I could spend more time together, and get to know each other like a real brother and sister should. I would call him when I got out of the hospital. When Aunt Terri, Uncle Jim, and Vivi came back into the room they were concerned. "Honey, are you alright? It has been a very trying day. Maybe you should get some rest" Vivi said. "I think she will be fine, just fine," Uncle Jim joined in. He had the saddest look on his face. "Uncle Jim, will you sing me to sleep?" I asked. "Of course I will, Babygirl. What do you want to hear?" he replied. "Anything," I said. He climbed up on the bed next to me, held me in his big strong arms, and sang *Jesus Loves the Little Children* until I drifted off to sleep. It was the best sound in the whole wide world.

When I woke up the next day, Uncle Jim, Aunt Terri and Vivi were all there looking after me. Vivi looked like she was doing paperwork, Aunt Terri was taking a nap, and Uncle Jim was playing solitaire. It was clear they were not going anywhere. Aunt Terri had spent the night with me at the hospital, and Uncle Jim decided he would work third shift to stay busy. He spent the morning sleeping, then came to the hospital in the afternoon. Vivi spent as much time as she could with me, but she was a busy lawyer, and her clients were demanding. She made sure to visit me every day, and always had a surprise for me. She had discovered my love for Kit Kats, and began bringing me one daily despite getting the business from the nurses. This continued over the next few days, and then the doctor finally said I could go home. News had spread about my attack, and people I didn't even know had sent me beautiful flowers. I had cards from the kids in my VBS class, and there was even one from Marvin. Aunt Terri said he had called a few times, and his mother brought him by the hospital to see me, but I was sleeping. Maybe he felt guilt for not speaking up for me when those girls were picking on me. I told myself that Marvin was a nice boy, and he did not know what to do to defend me, and that was the reason he didn't do or say anything. I was ok with that because boys should not fight girls' battles. When the doctor finally came to sign the release forms, I was more than ready to go home. It felt like I was there for at least a month, but it was only five days. The doctor kept me so long to ensure I did not get an infection in my stitches.

The first thing I wanted when I got home was a bath. The nurses gave me sponge baths daily, but I felt dirty. Aunt Terri said I would have to be careful because I had stitches still in my belly. The other stitches from my pocketbook were gone. The doctor said they came out on their own. I was still pretty sore down there, and Aunt Terri had to help me in and out of the tub. She also had to help me stand up and sit down. I felt like a little baby, but she warned me that if I tore my stitches it would be pretty painful. I was extremely careful because I did not want any more pain. After my bath, I put on my pjs and got into bed. Uncle Jim made me some of his famous chicken noodle soup. It was Grandma Rose's recipe, but Uncle Jim said he put his own spin on it. He promised to show me how to make it when I was all better. While Uncle Jim was in the kitchen, Aunt Terri braided my hair. She made these fancy swirls of corn rolls that went to the back of my head. I looked like an African Princess when she was finished. I was on the road to recovery, and I felt safe and loved. That's all I have really wanted since Daddy died.

Chapter 12: Books and Lessons Learned

Even though my body was healing, I still had a long way to go. I was pretty sore from the surgery, and I was having pain in my pocketbook area. Aunt Terri took me to the doctor for a checkup, and the doctor said this was normal for someone who had been through the trauma I had. She said I should expect sharp pains to come and go, but it would not happen very often. I was not very happy about that news, but I didn't have a choice. At least I was out of school for the summer, so I would have time to heal completely before having to deal with sitting in those hard, uncomfortable desks at school.

Since I needed something to occupy my time during my summer break, I decided to ask Aunt Terri what she thought I should do. She thought I should take it easy because of everything that happened, but I wanted to forget it ever took place. I felt the need to escape reality, and did not want to talk about it with anyone. Aunt Terri suggested that I see a friend of hers that taught Psychology at her college. All I heard her saying was, I was crazy. I saw people on TV who saw psychologists and called them head shrinkers. "Aunt Terri, I don't want anyone to shrink my head," I said with caution. Aunt Terri laughed and explained to me, "Butterfly, they don't actually shrink your head. They are counselors who you talk to about your problems, and they help make things better." "Does that mean that I am crazy now?" I asked. "No, baby, it just means that my friend is someone that you can talk to about all the feelings you are having about what happened to you. You can also talk about losing your dad, and the issues you have with your mom. She will be like a good friend who you can tell your secrets, and she will give you advice." Aunt Terri made it sound appealing, but I still did not want to talk to this lady. "Can I think about it, Aunt Terri?" I asked. "Sure, I don't want to push it on you if you are not comfortable, but promise me you will think about it," she replied. I shook my head to say I would think about it, but my mind was already made up; no head shrinker for me!

I wanted to avoid any further conversations about going to see doctors to talk about my so-called issues. I wanted to escape reality so that I did not have to think about anything. If I found something to do by myself, I would not have to talk to anyone, and then Aunt Terri would not have a reason to ask me to get my head shrunk. I decided to turn to my best friends in the whole wide world: books! I've noticed that no matter who you are or what age you are, nobody interrupts you when you are reading. People seem to have an unwritten rule about this. When you see someone with a book or magazine it just doesn't seem right to bother them. Since I have already read my small collection of book a hundred times, I asked Aunt Terri if she would take me to the library to get some different ones.

While I was in the Summer Reading Program, I heard these ladies talking about Edgar Allan Poe. They were talking about his dark and mysterious stories and poems. For some reason, this made me want to read more of his stuff, but I was too young to check it out of the library. I decided to beg Aunt Terri to check his books out for me. She hardly ever said no to me, and hopefully she would not start now. "No, Butterfly, absolutely not," Aunt Terri answered when I asked for the book. "But Aunt Terri, it's free. You wouldn't have to spend any money at all. It's not like I am asking you to buy it for me, I just want to borrow it for a while," I pleaded. "That writer is too adult for you. You should be reading about happy things. Poe is dark, and you are way too young to experience such things," she replied. "After the year I have had, how much darker can it get?" I wondered out loud. "I said no, and I mean it. Don't ask me again for at least two years," she barked. With that, the conversation was over. I knew better than to keep pushing the issue. As far as Aunt Terri was concerned, Poe was the devil, and I was not going to read him in her house.

I still needed some books to occupy my time, so I convinced Aunt Terri to take me to the library to get some age appropriate reading. "Aunt Terri, have you ever heard of Judy Blume?" I asked. "She's very popular among kids your age. I think she would be a good choice for you," Aunt Terri answered. She was happy that I liked to read, and was even happier to give me her opinions of my choices. That afternoon I checked out *Are you There God? It's Me Margaret* and *Iggie's House* by Judy Blume. I had a good feeling about those two books. I also checked out *Little House in the Big Woods* and *Little House on the Prairie* by Laura Ingalls Wilder. I watched the TV show for Little House, and I thought the books would be good too. I just loved Laura and Pa's relationship because it reminded me of Daddy and me. Only Laura had a great mom and good sisters that loved her. I was super excited to get home and read my books.

On the way home, Aunt Terri asked me questions that I had never thought about. "Butterfly, when you read those books of yours, can you see yourself being one of the characters? Do you think the people in the book would be your friends? Can you see yourself doing what they do?" she asked. I wasn't sure what she meant. The books were meant to tell the character's story, so I was confused. "Why would I see myself in the books? I am reading about the people that the author wants me to read about," I said without missing a beat. Was she trying to say I didn't make a good choice with the books I got today? "Butterfly, I want you to be able to put yourself in the main character's place. If you can do this, then you are really feeling what the author has written. If you can't do this, then maybe you should expand your choices. That's all. Just some questions for you to think about as you read. When you are finished with each book, I want you to answer those questions for me. Okay?" I never thought about it like that before, and it sounded like a challenge for me to learn something new. I decided to take the challenge. "Okay, Aunt Terri, you have a deal," I proclaimed.

When we got home, I tried to run into the kitchen, and read in my nook that Daddy shared with me, but Aunt Terri was not having it. "Butterfly, why don't you come sit at the table with me while I make myself some tea. I want to talk to you." All I wanted to do was go hide in my safe place and read my books. I hoped she didn't start that head shrink business again. "Aunt Terri, I really want to get started reading my books," I said in a whiny voice. "This will only take a few minutes, and besides, you have a whole three weeks to read those books," she answered. I sat at the table expecting some sort of lecture or another request to go talk to her friend. "So in the car I asked you those questions because I want you to dig deeper when you are reading. I know right now you read just for fun, but it's time you start to read for content. In every book there is an underlying lesson that the writer wants you to learn. I want you to practice this with the library books you have. I am also going to take you to Raleigh with me in a couple of weeks. While we are there we'll go to a local book store, and you can choose some books to add to your personal collection," she said. My eyes lit up, and I was filled with excitement. There was nothing I would rather do than go to a book store. I had never been to one, but I always wanted to go. The closest I'd been was the RIF truck at school. Every other Wednesday a man came to school with a big truck of books. We ordered books that we liked, and then a couple of weeks later our orders would come in, and we got to read all afternoon. Daddy always gave me money for the RIF man, and I loved getting the books, but I hated waiting for the orders to come back. Now I could actually go to a real book-store, purchase books, and that same day take them home.

"Really Aunt Terri, I can actually pick out my own books, and bring them home to keep?" I squealed. "Yes, Butterfly, but keep in mind they have to be age appropriate," Aunt Terri almost took the wind out of my sails. I was already scheming to get a Poe book, but she shut me down quickly. "Besides, the store I am taking you to doesn't sell Edgar Allan Poe," she said. I wondered how she knew what I was thinking, and what kind of bookstore didn't carry Poe. I really didn't care, I just wanted to get to the store and look around. I know they would have all kinds of treasures for me to discover. First I had to read my library books, and I chose to start with *Are You There God? It's Me Margaret,* and it didn't disappoint.

After reading the entire book, I asked myself if I could be Margaret. We had some things already in common, but there were more differences than things in common. I talked to God all of the time, but I never asked if he was there. Grandma Rose told me I would never be alone because God would always be right beside me. I was not confused about being a Christian like she was, because that was all I knew. I did have the same questions about bras, boys, and periods though. I determined that I could see myself as the main character, and this was a good book for me. When I told Aunt Terri she was pleased with my outcome. She said from now on, whenever I read a book, I should always ask myself these questions and more. She encouraged me to come up with my own set of questions and told me I should use the journal I won in the reading program to write down my answers. "If you're going to be a writer you are going to have to start writing. What better way to start?" she asked. I thought it was a great idea, and rushed upstairs to start writing my thoughts. I started writing, and before I knew it, I had filled up ten pages, and Aunt Terri was calling me to come downstairs to help with dinner. I had been reading and writing all afternoon, and I did not realize what time it was. Uncle Jim would be home soon, and I couldn't wait to tell him all about my day. Maybe later after dinner he would sing to me, and he and Aunt Terri could dance. I loved to watch them dance together. They loved each other so much, and my parents never did anything together. I was so thankful that they agreed to take care of me, and I did not want them to leave me. I constantly felt like I had to be the best child in the world, because I was afraid they would get tired of me and leave. Sometimes I still cried for my daddy, and sometimes I still missed my mommy. I would never tell anyone I missed her because she was so mean to me. I wondered what was wrong with me. Why did I think about her sometimes? Should I be ashamed that I wanted her in my life even though she hated me?

Chapter 13: Nightmares Come and Nightmares Go...

I was having trouble sleeping, and I did not know why. Yes, it was hot, but I had a box fan in my bedroom window, and it worked very well. We didn't have air conditioning upstairs so we used fans. Downstairs in the living room we had an air conditioning unit in the window. It made a lot of noise, but it cooled off most of the downstairs. Aunt Terri said heat rises, and she was sure telling the truth. If we did not turn on the fans, it was impossible to sleep. Tonight the heat wasn't the problem. My problem was every time I closed my eyes I felt like I was in a horror movie. I got chills down my spine, and I was very afraid of something or someone, but I could never see who or what. It never failed, as soon as my eyes shut I heard someone laughing at me, calling me names, and I couldn't take it. I wanted to sleep, but couldn't so I began reading with my flashlight. Uncle Jim must have seen the light underneath the door because he came in my room to check on me.

"Babygirl, are you alright? You're supposed to be sleeping, not reading. Don't make me take that flashlight," he warned. "I'm sorry, Uncle Jim. I am having trouble sleeping, so I decided to read until I fell asleep." "What's going on? Is it too hot for you up here? I'll tell you what, why don't you come downstairs with me where it's cool. We can watch TV and have a snack. It will be fun. What do you say?" he said. "I say yes!" I was excited because I never got to stay up late before in my life. I always had a strict bedtime, and there was never any negotiating. We stayed up until the wee hours of the morning watching TV, and eating junk. I must have eaten a pound of Twizzlers and a whole bag of Bugles. Those were my favorite snacks, and I always bugged Aunt Terri to buy them when we went to the store. Uncle Jim said he would replace them so Aunt Terri wouldn't find out that we stayed up. It was 2:00 in the morning, and the TV stations were off of the air. Uncle Jim insisted that I go to bed, because we would both get busted by Aunt Terri if she woke up, and he wasn't in the bed. "Babygirl, it's time. I hope you're good and sleepy because I sure am. I have to go to work in the morning, and I am going to be dragging," he said. We both went upstairs, and as I closed my bedroom door, I saw Aunt Terri waiting for him. "Jim what were you doing?" she asked. "Baby, I was in the bathroom," he lied. I laughed as I fell into bed, and listened to my aunt and uncle talking. Their voices must have lulled me to sleep because the next thing I knew Aunt Terri was waking me up.

"Come on, sleepy-head get your butt out of that bed," she sang. "I'm sleepy, Aunt Terri," I whined. "That's what happens when you stay up all night watching TV," she laughed. I guess Uncle Jim got busted when I was asleep. I hope he wasn't in too much trouble for letting me stay up. I dragged myself out of the bed, and Aunt Terri sprung a great surprise on me. "Today is the day! We are going to Raleigh, and you get to go to the bookstore!!!" Aunt Terri was giddy and excited. You would have thought I was taking her somewhere instead of the other way around. When I heard the surprise I immediately woke up. I jumped up off the bed and ran to the closet to see what I was going to wear. I grabbed a cute sundress, which was the first thing I saw, some underwear, and ran to the bathroom to take a quick bath. I heard Aunt Terri laughing at me as I shut the bathroom door. "Oh you're not so sleepy now, are you?" she giggled. I didn't care if she laughed; all I wanted was to hit the road. It took about an hour to get to Raleigh, and I did not want to waste any time. As we were driving to the city, Aunt Terri decided she would take advantage of the time, and ask me a question she was dying to ask but was afraid. "Butterfly, do you have nightmares about what happened to you in the park?" she wanted to know. I was afraid to tell her yes because I did not want her to take me to the shrink, but I needed to talk to someone. "Yes, Aunt Terri. When I close my eyes it feels like someone is after me, but I can't see who it is. I am afraid, and I don't want to go to bed. I only sleep when I am too tired to stay up anymore," I poured my heart out to her. "Why didn't you tell me this was going on?" she demanded. "Because, I don't want to get my head shrunk, and I know you are going to force me to go," I replied. "Zora, I will never force you to do anything you don't want to, but I still think it would help you to talk with someone," "Aunt Terri, can I just come talk to you when I need to? I trust you, and I don't want to talk to a stranger about my personal things. It's hard to say them out loud, and since you already know what happened, I don't have to repeat it." I made such a good case that Aunt Terri gave up trying to convince me to see a professional, at least for now. "Okay baby, I will drop it, and I want you to know that you can talk to me about anything. I want you to feel comfortable telling me about all of your thoughts and fears. I promise not to judge you, and you can speak candidly," she said. "Thank you," I said. I was extremely happy to change the subject because I hated thinking about what happened.

Once we arrived in Raleigh, we started out on the campus of NCSU. Aunt Terri took me to her office, and I met some of her colleagues. Her office was full of African American books, art, and tapestries. It was just like I had imagined it. One thing I wasn't expecting was the beautiful zebra print chair behind her desk. It was huge like you would see in a castle, and I instantly fell in love. I rushed to the chair as soon as I saw it, and discovered not only was it zebra print, it was made of actual zebra hide. It was so soft and plush, and I never wanted to get out of it. The arms were tall, and the knobs on the end were made out of the zebra's hooves! It was the best thing I had ever seen. Aunt Terri said she purchased it at an African store that she frequented in California, and it was her favorite piece of furniture on earth. She was told the zebra died of natural causes, so she wasn't freaked out about them using the hide. There was a red pillow in the chair that felt soft, but looked like coarse hair. The color scheme matched the school colors perfectly, and Aunt Terri said I looked great sitting in her chair.

Aunt Terri had a staff meeting to attend so she told me to hang out in her office while she was gone. There were so many books on her shelves I didn't know which one to choose first. After searching, I finally settled on a coffee table book with photographs of beaches in Jamaica. I got lost in the beauty of the pages, and did not hear him come in. There he was standing right in front of me once again. When did he get out of jail? How did he know where I was? Had he been following me all this time? I did not know what to do, but I knew for sure that he would not hurt me again. Uncle Jim had prepared me if anyone else tried to bother me, and I knew what to do this time. "What are you doing here?" I asked. He just stood there staring at me with those cold eyes. He finally spoke in a low deep voice, "I've been watching you. I bet you thought you got rid of me, but I'm back!" I guess he was trying to scare me, but those days were over. I picked up the book I was reading, and I slung it at his head. "Get out of here and don't come back," I screamed. That surprised him, and he was too slow to move out of the way. The book grazed his head, and he cursed at me. "You little bitch, I'm gonna beat you senseless," he yelled. Before he had a chance to rush at me, I picked up a statue of Martin Luther King, and threatened to brain him. He rushed me, and I moved out of the way. He fell into the desk, and I kicked him in his butt. I didn't give him a chance to grab me this time. I used the statue of Dr. King to bash his head, neck, and back. Dr. King may have been non-violent, but I wasn't! I struck him over and over until he fell to the floor. He was bleeding and screaming, and I could smell the alcohol on his breath. I was screaming at him to leave, and he finally did. As he crawled across the room towards the door, I kicked him one last time in the behind. He got to his feet, and stumbled down the hallway. I watched from the window as he got into the passenger side of Teresa Langston's car, and as the car drove off, I saw her in the driver's seat.

After I was sure they were gone, I climbed up into the zebra chair, and started praying. I asked God to keep me safe from this crazy man and his wife. As I was praying a strange calm came over me, and I knew everything would be alright. I didn't know how, but I knew it would be ok. I tried my best to clean up the mess in Aunt Terri's office before she returned from her meeting. I did not want to tell her what happened so I made sure to put everything back the way it was. All of the other professors were in the meeting with her so nobody saw or heard anything. When Aunt Terri returned she found me like she left me sitting in the zebra chair reading. There was a big difference though; my stomach was hurting very badly. "Aunt Terri, I don't feel very well," I said as she entered the room. "I want to go lie down," I continued. "What's wrong, Butterfly? You've been looking forward to this trip for a long time now. You must be sick. Do you want to go to the doctor?" she asked with concern. "No, I will be alright. I just want to go home." "What about the book store and the museum? We had a whole day planned." Aunt Terri was disappointed, but I could not get myself together enough to enjoy the bookstore. "Maybe next time," I said in with a weak voice. "Okay, maybe I should get you home. You don't look very good," she agreed. The ride home was long and awkward. It seemed like we would never get there. To avoid talking I pretended to be asleep, but all I saw when I closed my eyes was him.

As soon as we arrived at home, I raced upstairs to my room, and shut the door. I felt out of control, and did not know what to do. The only thing that made me feel better was reading. I needed to feel secure, so I decided to sit in my closet and read. He couldn't get me in my closet because I could see him coming. If I lost myself in this book, and he happened to come into my room, he would not expect me to be sitting in the closet. Somehow this made me feel better. I read so long that I guess I fell asleep because the next thing I knew Uncle Jim was standing over me as I was screaming. "Babygirl, wake up. It's Uncle Jim; I won't hurt you," he said. I was very scared, and I didn't know where I was at first. I was dreaming that Mr. Samuels had broken into the house and was beating me. "Uncle Jim, is that you?" I asked "You were having a bad dream, but you're ok now. What are you doing in the closet?" he demanded. "I was afraid Mr. Samuels would come back and get me, so I hid in the closet," I said. The look on Uncle Jim's face was something I never saw before. He looked angry, sad, hurt, and evil all at the same time.

"Babygirl, it's time for dinner. Do you feel well enough to eat a little something?" he asked. Uncle Jim looked weird, and I felt like there was something wrong with him, but I didn't know what. "I guess I could eat something," I replied. "Your Aunt wants you to wash your hands, and come down for dinner. You go ahead, and I will be right there," he instructed. As I walked to the bathroom to wash up for dinner, I felt sick to my stomach. I knew something bad was coming, and I knew I would be at the center of the storm. That night while we ate dinner there was an eerie silence at the table. We continued our normal routine after dinner, and while I washed dishes, Uncle Jim dried them. Usually we would joke and laugh, but not tonight. Tonight no one was in the mood for fun and games. Uncle Jim was a mile away lost in his thoughts. I was a little afraid to say anything because he looked on the verge of snapping. After finishing the dishes, I decided it was best to skip my hour of watching TV and go to bed.

When I reached the top of the stairs, I heard Uncle Jim ask Aunt Terri what happened today when we went to Raleigh. "Did something happen to her today? She doesn't seem right," he said. "I don't know," Aunt Terri replied. "What do you mean you don't know? Weren't you with her? It was your idea to take her to the school and expose her to these so-called intelligent people, and she comes back all messed up," Uncle Jim argued. "I told you, she was fine until I went to my staff meeting. When I came back the room looked fine, but it smelled like cleaning supplies, and there was a paper towel with blood on it in the trash. She said she was very sick and wanted to go home. When I asked if everything was alright she said her stomach hurt. She pretended to be asleep on the way home so I left her alone," Aunt Terri replied. "Well who was in the office when you left? Who had access? Something happened, and I want to know what!" he yelled. "Look, Jim, don't yell at me. There wasn't anyone else in the building. The students were in class, and all of the professors were in the meeting with me. I thought it was safe to leave her there." Then I heard Uncle Jim say, "There's only one way to know for sure. I am going up there to ask her point blank. I can't protect her if I don't know what happened. Did I tell you she was hiding in the closet when I went to get her for dinner? She had fallen asleep, and when I went in there she was having a nightmare about what that bastard did to her. I'm going up there right now to get the whole story." Then Aunt Terri said, "Jim, remember she's just a little girl. Don't lose your temper in front of her, or she will shut down, and never tell you anything else." I panicked when I heard his footsteps on the stairs and ran into the bathroom. When I came out I was surprised to see Uncle Jim waiting in my room for me. "Babygirl, what is wrong tonight? You have been acting funny all night, and I need to know if something happened to you today." "Nothing, Uncle Jim, I'm fine, really," I lied. I guess my lie was not good enough because he kept badgering me. "Look, you and me are supposed to be buddies right? Buddies always tell each other the truth no matter what. I know something happened today, and no matter what it was, I promise you I won't judge you. You can tell me and you can trust me," he said. "I'm scared, Uncle Jim. What if you get angry?" I whined. "Babygirl, you have to tell me no matter what. It's my job to protect you, and if you don't tell me when you are in danger I can't keep my promise to you. You remember I promised I would never let anyone else hurt you, right? Well if you don't tell me when someone is bothering you, I can't help." That was enough to start the river of words flowing out of my mouth. I told him everything that happened in Aunt Terri's office, and he just sat there taking it all in. He never said one word. When I finished, he stood up and walked toward to the bedroom door. As he was about to leave he turned to me and said, "You don't ever have to worry about him coming back again," in a low calm voice. When I looked up again, he was gone.

The next day as I was helping Aunt Terri clean up the living room, there was a knock on the door. I opened the door, and there stood Vivi! I was so excited to see her that I flung the door open, and gave her the biggest hug ever. "Hi Zora, how have you been? I missed you so much," she said. "Vivi, it's so good to see you. Are you gonna stay for dinner?" I asked. Vivi was not there just to see me; she had big news to share. Aunt Terri welcomed her, "Hi Vivi, won't you come in as soon as Zora stops cutting off your circulation?" We all laughed, and I released my kung fu grip on Vivi. She came in, and told us she had some news about Mr. Samuels. This morning he was found in the same park where he attacked me. He had been beaten within an inch of his life, and was in the hospital in a coma. Since Teresa Langston was now his wife, she was his next of kin, and decided to remove him from life support. He was dead!

Chapter 14: Christmas in July

Without knowing it, Teresa Langston had saved me from my tormentor. She let him die for her own selfish reasons, but I was grateful for the relief. I knew it was wrong to be happy that someone was dead, but I could not force myself to feel bad. After all of the time and energy he spent trying to destroy me, it was better for the world if this evil man was no longer walking around. It was just like the Bible verse that we learned in VBS: *"What you gain by doing evil won't help you at all, but being good can save you from death."* If Mr. Samuels had been a nice person, maybe Teresa Langston would have saved him from death. She didn't even wait a whole day before pulling the plug, which must mean he was extra evil.

Regardless of the drama going on around me, I decided I was finally going to be happy. I started saying my prayers every night like Daddy taught me, and I was now able to sleep. No more nightmares!!! I was so thankful the first time I slept through the night that I got up early, and made breakfast for Uncle Jim and Aunt Terri. In the back of my head I thought Uncle Jim may have had a hand in getting rid of Mr. Samuels. He was so angry when I told him about what happened at the school, and he swore to protect me. I didn't care if he did hurt Mr. Samuels because he did it out of love. I'm not saying Uncle Jim had anything to do with it, but a little piece of me hopes he did. The thought made me feel safe, like nobody in the whole world would ever bother me again. I liked that feeling, and I did not want anyone to take it away.

After washing the breakfast dishes I asked Aunt Terri for a big favor. I was scared she would say no, but I really wanted this. "Aunt Terri, can we go back to Raleigh today? I really want to go to the bookstore and the museum." She looked surprised and Uncle Jim chuckled, "Terri you should take her considering the hard time she has had lately." "I would be happy to take her, but remember Jim, you have a doctor's appointment today and I have to take you," Aunt Terri replied. "How about this, I join you pretty ladies on your road trip, and we'll have an adventure together?" Uncle Jim said. "Don't play with me, Jim. I know you're just trying to avoid your doctor's appointment. I'll tell you what, you can come with us after you see the doctor," Aunt Terri replied. I started laughing because she always had his number.

After Uncle Jim saw the doctor, the three of us headed to Raleigh for a day of fun and adventure. Truth be told, I was happy Uncle Jim took the day off, and we all could have a family day out of the house for a change. Usually it was just Aunt Terri and me. I enjoyed when my uncle was around. He was so funny, and he always knew how to have a good time. He reminded me of my Daddy, but he was also very different. Daddy loved to read, and was more quiet and reserved like me. Uncle Jim was the life of the party, and his passion was music. He would sing all day long if Aunt Terri would let him. Luckily today she was in the mood for music, so we sang and laughed all the way to Raleigh. We went to the Museum of History first, and I got to see so many historical events that took place in North Carolina way before I was even thought of. It was nice to learn about the past, and see how far my state has come since then. I learned an interesting tidbit about my school. Apparently it served as a hospital in the Civil War, and many soldiers died there. There were pictures of the school, and it looked pretty much the same then as it does now. I wondered if any of the rooms were haunted by the ghosts of the dead soldiers. I would ask my new teacher when I returned next month. When we left the museum, Uncle Jim was starving, so we decided to have lunch. "Babygirl, what do you want to eat?" he asked. I did not know what I wanted, but I didn't want him to know that so I said, "I think I'm in the mood for pasta." That was always my go to food when I did not know what I wanted because I could eat Italian food every-day, just not spaghetti. "Big surprise; you always want pasta," Uncle Jim laughed. "Well, let's see what we have around here. Terri, do you know this area of town?" he continued. "There's a place just down the block. I heard it was pretty good, but I have never eaten there" Aunt Terri announced. "Well let's go! Come on Babygirl, let's get us some pasta" Uncle Jim sang.

As we walked to the restaurant I realized that I was really happy for the first time in a very long time. I said a little prayer that it could always be this way. At the restaurant I ordered something called baked ziti with sausage. I did not know exactly what it was, but the description sounded delicious. It came with a salad and garlic bread. Uncle Jim ordered something with seafood in it that smelled nasty, and Aunt Terri had a salad. "Terri, really, who goes to an Italian restaurant and eats a salad?" Uncle Jim picked on Aunt Terri. "You like my curves where they are, don't you? If you want them to spread, I'll go ahead and order the lasagna," Aunt Terri chimed in. "Baby you would look good no matter what; you know you bad" Aunt Terri giggled, and Uncle Jim rubbed his hand on her thigh. I loved watching how they showed each other affection. There was no question that he adored her, and she would do anything for him. That's how a real family should be…happy.

After lunch Uncle Jim wanted to stop in this record store that we passed on the way to the restaurant. As soon as we entered I knew he was in heaven. There was a wall full of posters of famous singers and musicians. Uncle Jim used to be in a band when he lived in California, and he always took advantage of any musical situation. I knew he loved music like I did books, and we could be in this store for hours if he had gotten loose. I liked listening to his stories about meeting famous people or seeing such and such in concert. His face lit up, and he was lost in another world. Aunt Terri was not as enthused as I was, and decided she would browse on her own. One of the artists that he loved so much was named Bob Marley, and he went on and on about him. Uncle Jim saw him in concert several times, but his most memorable was on July 9, 1975 at the Roxy Theatre in Los Angeles. "I'll never forget it, Zora, it was magical. The man was amazing. He did not need an opening act, and nobody closed for him; just him, the band, and the music. It was the way he sung that struck me so much. You could tell he loved what he did, and it wasn't for the money. It was the best $8 I have ever spent," he recalled. Uncle Jim broke out with his rendition of *I Shot the Sherriff* and started doing this weird little dance. I laughed, and that must have brought him back to his senses. He was lost in his memories. "Your Aunt Terri looked so beautiful that night. I knew as soon as I saw her that she would be my wife. I fell in love at first sight. So you see, Babygirl, if it wasn't for Bob Marley, I would never have met your Aunt Terri." He told the story with big dreamy eyes, and before he could finish, he walked across the room, swung Aunt Terri around, and planted a big kiss on her lips. She was surprised, but I could tell she liked it very much. They looked at each other like they were teenagers in love. "Jim, let's get out of here, and take Zora to the bookstore before it closes," Aunt Terri said while blushing.

When we arrived at the bookstore I almost lost my mind. I had never seen so many books in my life. I did not know where to begin, and I was running back and forth until Aunt Terri grabbed my arm, "Butterfly, calm down, those books aren't going anywhere." "Aunt Terri, I can't help it. There are so many books, and I want to read them all! Where do I start?" I said with excitement. "Babygirl, I knew you loved to read, but I had no idea you liked books this much," Uncle Jim laughed. "Here, why don't you start in the children's section, and when you are finished there we will move on to poetry, Okay?" Aunt Terri suggested. That was just fine with me. Aunt Terri and Uncle Jim said I could choose as many books as I wanted with one exception: I had to be able to carry them out of the store myself. They sat in the corner at a table drinking coffee, and whispering in each other's ears while I shopped.

I must have spent over 30 minutes trolling through the stacks of children's books before I found just the right ones. I chose Clifford the Big Red Dog and Curious George. I had seen these books when the man from RIFF came to my school, but I had not gotten to purchase them yet. I also found several books that had collections of poems by African American poets including Gwendolyn Brooks, Nikki Giovanni, and Langston Hughes. One of the poems that really stuck out was *We Real Cool* by Gwendolyn Brooks. I also chose a book of poems by Edgar Allen Poe; Aunt Terri decided to lift her ban on Poe, and she let me get it. I was so excited to have so many books to read. It was like Christmas had come early this year, and I couldn't wait to get home and organize my new library additions. I was on cloud nine, and Uncle Jim was super happy too. We laughed and sang songs, and danced all the way home.

Aunt Terri drove us back to Goldsboro, and since we had a long day she decided we could have pizza for dinner. I could tell Uncle Jim enjoyed spending time with us, and he especially enjoyed his time with Aunt Terri. They spent the evening after dinner shut up in their bedroom playing music, and doing stuff that grown people do in the dark. I organized my new books, and decided to read a book of poems until I drifted off to sleep. This was the best night I could remember having in this house since Daddy died. Everything seemed to be looking up. Maybe, just maybe, God would answer my prayers and let it stay like this forever.

Chapter 15: Birthday Cake

The summer was going by very quickly, and my birthday was at the end of the week. I could not believe I would be turning 10 years old. I was very excited that my birthday was almost here. The 4th of July was fun, but the 7th was the day I wanted to celebrate. I loved my birthday, and this year it fell on a Saturday. I always got a cake, a new book, and I got to choose what I wanted for dinner. One thing Teresa Langston was known for was celebrating her children's birthdays. Even though she hated me, she always threw me a big dinner party for my birthday. There was always a lot of decorations, and she made these beautiful invitations for the people she invited; mostly her friends and their children because I did not have any friends of my own. It usually turned out to be a big deal with me hiding upstairs in my room until it was time to eat. Every year she asked me what kind of cake I wanted, and no matter what I said she would always get me a chocolate cake with chocolate icing. I loved chocolate, but I grew to hate chocolate cake because of her. It was her way of letting me know that even if it was my birthday, she still was in control, and she hated me. None of that mattered because I had Daddy. He always made my day special because he loved me so much.

Every year on my birthday, Daddy would wake me up with pancakes in bed. I was never allowed to eat food in my room, but he always made an exception on my birthday. Daddy would eat breakfast with me, and then he would give me a present. Each year he gave me a pretty dress with matching shoes and hair bows. He said that every little girl should feel like a princess on her special day. I would take a bath, and get dressed while Daddy cleaned up the kitchen, and then we would head out for the day before anyone had a chance to wake up. He let me choose where I wanted to go, and we would hang out all day. Daddy knew how much I loved birthday cake, so he always took me to this bakery on Center Street where he knew the owner. My favorite cake was carrot cake, and he would get the owner to bake us one just for two people. She always had a table decorated with all this pretty china and tea sets. We would eat our cake, and drink tea from fancy china. I felt like the most special girl in the world. Since we had to keep it a secret from the rest of the family, we had to eat the entire cake before we left, which wasn't a problem. The lady at the bakery always took 2 Polaroid pictures of us; one for me and one for him. Daddy kept the most current picture in his wallet, and I kept all of mine in a shoe box that I decorated with glitter and construction paper. I kept the shoe box hidden in the back of my closet. For as long as I could remember we had this ritual, but this year I would be sad because he was gone, and I would never be his little princess again. I treasured the memories he gave me, and I have my tiaras that he bought for me as reminders. I have one for each year we were together, and they are on a shelf in my room above my bed. He told Teresa Langston that they were my birthday gifts, and she believed him. My real gift was him showing me how much he loved me, and letting me choose my own flavor of birthday cake. During my party at home I always wore my tiara and looked at my pictures when I was hiding in my room before dinner. This year for my present I am going to ask Aunt Terri for picture frames so I could hang my memories on the wall. I knew just where to put them, right underneath the tiaras.

When I came downstairs for breakfast, Aunt Terri greeted me with a big hug. "Good morning, Butterfly. How are you today?" she asked. "Morning, Aunt Terri, I am well and you?" I responded with a happy tone. "There are only 2 days left before your birthday. What would you like to do to celebrate?" she sang. "I don't know, Aunt Terri, but I know what I want for my present. "Oh and what is that?" "I would like to have some picture frames so I can hang these pictures of me and Daddy on my bedroom wall," I answered. I decided I would show Aunt Terri my pictures, and ask her for help with picking out the perfect frames. "Oh Butterfly, these are precious. When did you take them?" she inquired. I explained to Aunt Terri about Daddy's special gift that he gave me every year, and I got lost in my words. When I snapped back to reality, Aunt Terri was sitting at the table looking at me with big wide eyes crying. It was as if she was happy and sad all at the same time.

"What's wrong, Aunt Terri?" I asked. "Oh nothing, I just never realized how special a relationship you had with your daddy until now. You must miss him very much," she replied. "Yes, I do, but he gave me such good memories that I always go there in my mind when something bad happens. I don't think about what is happening; I just put myself with Daddy, and everything is alright." I must have said too much because Aunt Terri broke down crying, and had to leave the room. I didn't mean to make her sad. I just wanted some picture frames. I hope she doesn't want to leave now. I was scared that I would run her off with my stories, and I did not want that. From now on I would keep them to myself. I needed her around, and Uncle Jim loves her so much that he would probably leave too, and I would be alone again. I ran behind her, and yelled, "Aunt Terri I'm sorry. I didn't mean to make you cry. Please don't leave me." She stopped dead in her tracks, and turned around to face me. I didn't know what she was going to do, but I was holding my breath. She ran down the stairs, and hugged the stuffing out of me. "Butterfly, you don't ever have to worry about me leaving you. I love you like you were my own child, and a real mother does not abandon her baby. The only way I will leave you is if God takes me, and I plan on living for quite some time." I smiled as she hugged me, and I felt loved and secure. I know now that she was the mother I always wanted and needed, and she would never leave me alone. "I love you, Aunt Terri," I said with a squeak in my voice. "I love you too, Butterfly. Now, let's stop all this crying, and get back to your birthday celebration," she answered.

We sat down in the living room, and devised a plan to celebrate my birthday. Aunt Terri decided that I should have an old-fashioned tea party! She would invite both ladies and gentlemen from the church, and people she knew that loved me. We would dress up in pretty dresses, and the guys would wear suits, and since this was a tea party, everyone would wear hats. Aunt Terri said this would be a good way to remember my daddy since he started the tradition. We decided to order the sweets from the bakery that Daddy always took me to. When we arrived at the bakery, the lady who owned it was happy to see me. "Hello, Zora, it's almost time to celebrate your birthday. I was wondering if I would hear from your father this week. You guys are cutting it close," she announced. "Yes, ma'am. You see, my daddy passed away a few months ago so I wasn't sure if I would be celebrating this year," I responded. The look on her face was very somber, and she said, "I am so sorry. I hadn't heard about your father. He was such a nice man, and he really loved you." I didn't know what else to say, so I told her the reason we were there. "This is my Aunt Terri, and she is giving me a tea party for my birthday. We need to order some sweets for the party." We ordered a bunch of pastries and when Aunt Terri asked what kind of cake I wanted, the lady said "Carrot cake is her favorite, and I make it for her every year." She was right, but I felt funny eating carrot cake without Daddy. It was our thing, and I did not want to share that with anyone else. "This year I would like to change things up a bit. I am turning 10, and I would like to have strawberry shortcake for my birthday," I announced. I read about a girl who loved strawberry shortcake in a book during the summer reading program. The girl in the book made it sound so delicious that I told myself I would try it if I ever got the chance. The owner of the bakery looked confused, but she agreed to make the cake. She promised to deliver the cake on the day of the party and Aunt Terri and I left to find decorations.

Aunt Terri and I went shopping, and she purchased supplies for the party. There were linen table cloths with matching napkins, lace doilies, and to top it off she purchased a beautiful tea set with this fancy tea that was imported from England. I had never had anything that was imported before, and it made me feel special. We also purchased some very pretty invitations that Aunt Terri and I handwrote and delivered personally to each person's house. Since it was such short notice there was not enough time to mail them. We did not invite a lot of people, but the ones we did accepted the invitation right away. Everyone in the neighborhood liked Aunt Terri and Uncle Jim and they all knew Aunt Terri really knew how to throw down in the kitchen. She said when she retired from the college she was going to open a little restaurant/bar in Jamaica where Uncle Jim could play his music, and she could cook. It sounded like paradise to me.

I was getting nervous about the girls she invited to come to the party. I liked their parents, but the girls and I were never friends. They thought I was weird, and I thought they were stuck up. I promised myself to be on my best behavior because I did not want to embarrass Aunt Terri and Uncle Jim. Maybe I would be able to get along with the girls. After all, we attended VBS together, and there weren't any problems then. Aunt Terri did not invite the mean girls from the church because I told her they were the reason I ended up walking through the park that day. She did, however, invite Marvin and his parents. Aunt Terri liked him and said he was a very respectful boy. He was nice to me after the attack, and we had spoken on the phone several times after. I was happy he was coming.

The morning of the 7th I woke up with a song in my heart. I jumped out of bed, and went to take a shower. When I returned to my room I found Uncle Jim waiting for me. "Good morning, Birthday Girl! I have a surprise for you," he chimed. "I love surprises. What is it?" I asked. He pointed to the tray full of pancakes on my desk. "Your daddy used to write me letters about your birthday celebrations, and had it written in his will for me to continue the tradition. I hope you don't mind." I didn't mind at all. He made me breakfast just like Daddy used to, and on my bed was a big white box wrapped with a beautiful yellow bow. I rushed over to the desk to eat my pancakes, and they looked delicious. Uncle Jim made enough for both of us so we ate together, while he sang me the Happy Birthday song.

After we ate, I washed my hands and ran to the bed to open the box. Inside was a beautiful yellow and white party dress with a matching hat, shoes, and gloves. I would get to look like a princess today after all. I was so excited that I rushed into Uncle Jim's arms and squeezed him so tight that I hurt my own arms. "I take it you like your present," Uncle Jim chuckled. "It's the most beautiful dress ever. Thank you so much," I exclaimed. "Don't thank me, Babygirl, thank your daddy. I was just following his instructions. Since you are having a tea party, Aunt Terri thought you should have a hat instead of the tiara. That way you can keep the tiara tradition between you and your daddy." I started crying, and Uncle Jim thought I was upset, but I was happy. How did Daddy know I would miss our special time on my birthday? For him to ask my uncle to continue doing this, meant so much to me. I felt very blessed to have such a great daddy and to be living with my aunt and uncle who truly loved me.

I went downstairs to thank Aunt Terri. She was in the kitchen working her behind off. There were all these different kinds of sandwiches with the crust cut off, and pasta salads with all kinds of ingredients. She made one of those tomato, onion and cucumber salads that you pour vinegar over, potato salad and a Watergate salad. She must have gotten up with the chickens because there was a ton of food in there. I don't know how Uncle Jim managed to make pancakes without getting in her way. "Aunt Terri, thank you so much for my beautiful dress. I love it," I exclaimed as I entered the kitchen. "You are very welcome. Happy Birthday, Butterfly," she answered happily. "Do you need any help in here?" I asked. "Not on your birthday, besides Vivi is coming over early to help me, and we will have this place looking good. Don't you worry," she said. "I do have something for you to do. I need you and your uncle to go to the store and get some things. I made a list, and it's right there on the fridge," she continued. "I'm on it!" I replied. I gave her a big hug, and then I ran back upstairs to tell Uncle Jim we had an assignment to go to the store. I think it was a way to get rid of us so we wouldn't be in her way.

Uncle Jim and I went on our assignment, but along the way we stopped at the auto store. Uncle Jim loved air fresheners, and he would never pass up a chance to buy a new one. We spent a good 15 minutes in the auto store picking out his favorite scents and then making the purchase. Then we went to the grocery store to buy the items on Aunt Terri's shopping list. We were almost finished when I heard the voice of Teresa Langston. She was shopping on the next aisle over, and the sound of her voice caused me to freeze in my tracks. I did not want to run into her ever again, but especially not on my birthday. Uncle Jim noticed that I stopped and wanted to know what was wrong "Babygirl, what's going on? We need to get this stuff back to Terri before I get scalped." "Shhhh!" I said. He looked at me like I had two heads, but did not say another word. Just then she crossed by the aisle that we were on. She did not see us, and we were able to get almost out of the store before she said anything. She was talking with her sister and running down Uncle Jim. "He thinks he better than me, and that wife of his ain't no prize. They think they are gonna keep me from all that money, but I got news for them. That's my child and my money. They can have her, but the money is mine!" She chattered on and on. Uncle Jim looked at me to see if I was ok, but I acted like I did not hear her. I already knew she didn't love me, so it no longer hurt when she said mean things. "Uncle Jim, let's go before Aunt Terri has a fit," I said. Just as we got to the door Teresa Langston said, "I know he was responsible for putting John in that coma. I can't prove it, but I know." She was loud and crazy, and I hated her for trying to hurt Uncle Jim. I was determined not to let her ruin my special day, so I said "Uncle Jim, I'll race you to the car." His face lit up, and we were off to the races. It was a temporary fix, but it worked.

As I was getting dressed for the party, Aunt Terri came into my room to help me. She said there was something missing from my outfit, and she knew just the thing. She handed me a box that was wrapped in beautiful paper and ribbons. As I opened the box she said, "Butterfly, every young lady needs to learn how to accessorize. I saw this in the store and thought it was perfect for you." I opened the box, and there was a gorgeous butterfly necklace. It was silver, and the stones were real turquoise and the antennae were covered with diamonds. I couldn't believe my eyes. No one had ever given me a present like this before. "Young ladies should have nice things, and I wanted to give you something that could last a lifetime. I hope you will wear it and know that I love you very much," Aunt Terri said as she fought back the tears. I hugged her and told her how much she meant to me. I wanted to wear this necklace every day for the rest of my life; it was so beautiful, and it meant that Aunt Terri and I would be together forever.

The party began promptly at 4:00 pm, the proper time for English tea, according to Aunt Terri. Everyone arrived a little early, and they were dressed to the nines. All the ladies had on yellow dresses and hats that matched, while the gentlemen wore dark suits with yellow ties and white shirts. I felt like an angel in my white dress with yellow trim, and I floated around the room welcoming our guests. Out of everyone there, Aunt Terri, Vivi and Uncle Jim were the sharpest. Aunt Terri out did herself with the decorations. There were several arrangements of yellow daisies and white roses on the table in addition to the beautiful china set that she had. The plates had little butterflies in the center, with matching tea cups and saucers that really set off the décor. She served tea to the children's table in a teapot that matched the china. The adult table had a silver tea pot and serving trays. Around the sides of the room she set up several small tables covered with linen table cloths and a host of food. I had never seen such a sight in my life. She really went all out, and to think all of this was just for me. The lady from the bakery had delivered the pastries, and Aunt Terry arranged them on these silver rounds with three tiers each. The cake was still in the kitchen and would be presented later during the party. Everyone fixed a plate, sat at their designated seats, and Uncle Jim said a blessing. Once we all had our fill and were good and fat, Uncle Jim announced it was time for the birthday cake! He had one more surprise for me. He had written a song birthday song just for me, and he sang it so beautifully. Aunt Terri brought the cake in from the kitchen while he was singing. The song made me cry because I felt loved and safe and home! Just as I was feeling the most joy I had felt in a very long time, the front door flung open, and there stood Teresa Langston holding the dreaded chocolate cake. Queenie and Big Willie were standing behind her looking ashamed. Apparently she heard about my party, and decided she would attend. "Zora, I'm here now. The party can begin! I don't know why you people are giving her that strawberry shortcake, because my child likes chocolate cake," she announced through her alcoholic haze.

I was horrified! Doesn't she know how to act? Why does she continue to torture me? Why can't she just go away, and leave me alone for good? I couldn't believe she showed up here, and embarrassed me in front of the people from church. I was finally getting along with the girls, and she had to come in and ruin that. I would never be happy as long as she was around, and I wanted her gone! Aunt Terri tried to diffuse the situation by inviting them in, but in typical Teresa Langston fashion, she escalated things. "Bitch, you've got some nerves inviting me into my own home. This is my house, and me and my kids are moving back in here right now." Big Willie pulled at her arm and said, "Mom, let's go. You're embarrassing us. You're drunk!" She swung around, and slapped him across the face. "Get your hands off of me, boy. I ain't going nowhere. This is my house. Mine! You hear me? You all get out!" she demanded. The guests started to leave, but Uncle Jim stopped them. Aunt Terri was fuming, and I knew I had to do something. I stood up and walked over to her and said, "Correction, this is MY house, and you are not welcome here. Take your nasty chocolate cake, and your nasty attitude and leave!" She was shocked and didn't know what to say, so she drew back and slapped me as hard as she could. That was the last straw. I saw Aunt Terri go in the side drawer of the end table, and pull out her hand gun. She cocked it and put it directly in between Teresa Langston's eyes at the same time moving me out of the way. "If you put your hands on this child again, it will be the last thing you do in life. Get your trashy ass out of here, and never come back. If you do, me and this Smith & Wesson will be waiting for you. You dig?" There was nothing left to say. Teresa Langston turned on her heels and left with her two oldest children in tow. She would not be back.

Chapter 16: Queenie Jumps Bad

After the big fiasco during my birthday party, the guests felt uncomfortable, and we understood when they wanted to leave. Aunt Terri apologized over and over again, and insisted that everyone at least take a piece of cake with them. I knew it would be a long time before people would get over this incident, and I was sure it ruined my chances of making any new friends. I felt bad that Teresa Langston destroyed all of Aunt Terri's hard work, but there was nothing I could do to repair it.

I spent the next week opening presents, writing thank you cards, and organizing my new toys. I couldn't believe all of the great gifts I received. To start there was the Farrah Fawcett Glamour Kit, Wonder Woman Underoos, Malibu Barbie and Ken dolls, A Kissing Christie doll, and Hungry, Hungry Hippo game. There were many more toys, but my favorite was the Snoopy Snow Cone Maker, and I couldn't wait to make those red and blue snow cones. I had so many new toys I had to find space for them in my room. I made it a point to handwrite a thank you note to all of my guests. Aunt Terri said it is very important to let your guests know you appreciate them and to make them feel as special as you felt opening the gift.

Things had been quiet around our house as Aunt Terri and Uncle Jim avoided talking about the spectacle that was made at the party. Neither of them wanted to discuss the fact that Aunt Terri threatened to kill Teresa Langston in front of the prominent members of the church because it was embarrassing. I, on the other hand, was very proud. I thought Aunt Terri was the baddest lady alive. She showed no fear and protected me like a lioness protecting her cub, and it made me smile every time I thought about it. I would be willing to bet nobody present on that day would be messing with me or Aunt Terri anytime soon. I had confined myself to the house for the last week and was getting a little stir crazy. I decided since it was so very hot outside I needed to cool off at the pool. We did not have our own swimming pool and did not know anyone who did, so I asked Aunt Terri to take me to the community pool at Mina Weil Park. That was the place to be on a hot summer day. I could not swim, but I loved to play in the shallow water and cool off. There was just one thing: I hated to get my hair wet because it took Aunt Terri forever to braid it. I usually wore a swim cap to prevent any accidents, but that made me look like an alien. The good thing was most of the other girls had the same issue, and nobody laughed at anyone else for wearing one.

"Aunt Terri, what are you doing today?" I asked as soon as I walked into the kitchen. "First and foremost, good morning," she corrected me. "I'm sorry, good morning, Aunt Terri," I apologized. "Now that your manners have returned, I really don't have any plans. What did you have in mind?" she replied. "I was hoping you would take me swimming at the park." Aunt Terri thought about it for a minute and then said, "I guess that would be ok, but I might make all those ladies at the pool jealous with all this fineness," she joked. "Woo Hoo! I'm going upstairs and put on my swimsuit right now!" I was so excited to go swimming that I forgot to ask Aunt Terri if she could swim. Surely she knew how to swim because she used to live in California, and I saw pictures of her playing in the ocean. Nobody would dare get in the ocean and not know how to swim.

When we arrived at the pool, Aunt Terri paid the entrance fee, and she took her spot at a poolside table in the shade. She pulled out her book and gave me a kiss. "Have fun, Butterfly, and remember I am right here if you need me." I played in the shallow end of the pool with the other kids and was having a great time until I had to go to the bathroom. Contrary to what you see on TV, most of the people I know do not pee in the pool. I left the pool and ran into the bathroom to do my business. As I was washing my hands I heard a familiar voice behind me.

"You think you are something, don't you? Well, you ain't shit; I hate you and I wish you were dead." I did not turn around, but looked in the mirror to see my sister Queenie standing there. I knew she hated me just like Teresa Langston, and I knew she would try to attack me if she ever got me alone, like now for instance. "Well Queenie, I'm sorry to hear that. I have always looked up to you and never understood why you disliked me" I responded. "You're sorry to hear that. You make me sick. You are the reason I had to move out of the only home I have ever known, and now I live in the projects. We are broke, and I don't have pretty dresses like the one you had at your party. In fact, I did not have a birthday party this year because mom couldn't afford it, and my dad was in jail. Do you know what it's like to have everyone in the neighborhood laughing at you?" she ranted.

"Actually I do and always have. What's happening to you has always been the case for me. As far as you leaving the house, blame that on your father. He was the one doing those bad things to me. I did not want him to touch me and make me put his thing in my mouth. I really did not want him to attack me in the park either," I said. "Don't even try it. You are the reason my dad is dead. If it wasn't for you, we could have lived happily ever after. You had a dad that loved you, and you took mine away," she accused. "Your father and mother killed my daddy, and don't blame me because your father was sick. Only a sick person would do what he did to a child. Your father got what he deserved and so will your mom." I knew I shouldn't have said that, but it was what I was thinking, and it just flew out of my mouth. Queenie's face tightened, and her eyes bulged out of her head. I could see she was super angry, and I knew that she would take a swing at me. I watched her in the mirror until I saw her arm twitch, and I ducked out of her way. She punched the mirror and cut her hand wide open. Blood was flowing everywhere, and she let out a blood-curdling scream. I could not tell if it was out of pain or anger, but I decided I would help her anyway. I grabbed some paper towels and wrapped her hand as she tried to pull away. "Don't help me, I hate you!" she screamed. Just then I grabbed her and said, "Hold still, there's glass in the cut." Queenie stopped fighting me and let me wash out her cut and wrap her hand in clean paper towels. There wasn't a first aid kit in the bathroom, so I did not have anything else.

"Why are you helping me when I just tried to punch you?" Queenie asked. "Because you're my sister, and I love you. I can't blame you for loving your father, but I don't think it's fair for you to blame me for what happened to him or you," I responded. "Forget you! I still hate you and wish you were dead," she confessed. With that, we walked out of the bathroom still enemies. I headed back to the pool while Queenie went to find a first aid kit and tell her mom what happened. As I was walking past the deep end of the pool, I saw Teresa Langston charging at me "You cut my baby! I'm going to kill you!" she screamed. Before I could react, she flew at me, and we both fell into the deep end of the pool. She pushed my head under the water and was trying to drown me. I panicked and was flailing around and thought I was dying when I saw Grandma Rose. She was so real and she said, "Don't worry Zora; I won't let anything happen to you. Today is not your day to die." Just then I felt Teresa Langston let go of my head, and I saw her and Aunt Terri fighting in the water. The next thing I knew, Queenie jumped in the pool and pulled me to safety. I couldn't believe it; Queenie actually saved me. People were panicking all over the place, and the life-guard helped Queenie and me out of the pool. Aunt Terri got away from Teresa Langston and ran over to make sure that I was ok.

Once she was convinced I was ok, she turned her anger toward Teresa Langston again. Before Aunt Terri could walk away I said, "Please don't leave me!" I was talking to Grandma Rose, but Aunt Terri thought I was talking to her and stopped in her tracks. She held my hand until the paramedics arrived. The police came and dragged Teresa Langston away in handcuffs. Queenie and Big Willie were standing there together looking lost. I asked Aunt Terri if they could stay with us until things were sorted out, but the police took them away too. After the paramedics checked me out and said it was all right for me to go home, I felt relieved. I said, "Aunt Terri, I need to learn how to swim." She smiled sadly, and shook her head. "Let's go home, Butterfly. Your uncle is going to have a fit."

Before we could leave a police detective came over to question us about what happened. I told him everything, and he assured me that I no longer had to worry about being tormented by her. "She will be going to jail for a very long time. She tried to kill you in front of dozens of witnesses, and they all tell the same story. This case is a slam dunk, but young lady you've got one crazy family." "Don't I know it," I replied sarcastically. How could I deny that my family was crazy; my own blood mother tried to kill me for money? What kind of evil dwelled in her? I wasn't sure, but I knew one thing it did not dwell in me. I would say a prayer for her tonight when I went to bed. I would also pray for Queenie and Big Willie. What would happen to them now? They had no one to look after them.

Chapter 17: Sibling Rivalry

After all of the drama at the pool, I started to think about my brother and sister and how they must feel with their father dead and their mother in jail. After all I had Aunt Terri and Uncle Jim to take care of me, and they seemed very happy to do it. Queenie and Big Willie did not have that. After they were taken away by the police, Aunt Terri told me they were in foster care for a couple of days, and then they went to live with Teresa Langston's sister, my Auntie Jen. Auntie Jen and Teresa Langston looked almost identical, and everyone thought they were twins. While they were sisters, Auntie Jen was younger by 11 months. She never married, but had a slew of eager men willing to pay her bills and buy her gifts. She played them like the fools they were and lived great doing it. Auntie Jen never finished high school because she said she would never need it; her beauty was going to take care of her, and when she got old she would still be fine! Her philosophy was: "There's always someone older than you, and old men love younger women." I felt sorry for her because she always seemed unhappy even though she had lots of things. She was always angry and did not eat the foods she loved because she did not want to lose her girlish figure. Auntie Jen hated me just as much as Teresa Langston did, and she was not shy about telling me. She was nicer to Queenie and Big Willie, but she was not mother material. She always said she hated kids and would get rid of them if she ever had any.

I wondered if my siblings would get the love they deserved living with Auntie Jen. She never really wanted us around and always complained that we were running off her men whenever she would babysit for us. I asked Aunt Terri, "Can I go visit my brother and sister?" "That's a random request. Where did this come from all of a sudden?" Aunt Terri asked. I couldn't explain why after all this time I wanted to see them, but I did. "I don't know, Aunt Terri. I guess seeing them at the pool and seeing how hurt they looked when the police took them away caused me to think about what they have been through. I realized I am not the only person Mr. Samuels hurt by attacking me," I said. "Are you sure they will want to see you? After all, Queenie did try to beat you up at the pool," she replied. "I know, but then she saved me from drowning. There must be some part of her that has feelings for me, or at the very least misses me. I know Big Willie cares for me because he told me in the hospital after he saved me at the park. I just think our parents tried to keep us apart, but I love my brother and sister." Aunt Terri said she would call to set up a time for us to get together, but I shouldn't get my hopes up.

Aunt Terri reached out to Auntie Jen to see if Queenie and Big Willie were even interested in seeing me, and the phone call was crazy from the half of the conversation I heard. Auntie Jen had the nerve to ask for gas money to bring them to the restaurant and requested that Aunt Terri pay for the meals. We wanted to meet in a public place so nobody would act out, but that didn't seem to matter much anymore. People seemed to be acting out anywhere they wanted these days, and nobody felt ashamed of their behavior. Aunt Terri was more than happy to pay for the meals, but the gas money was a bit much, so she suggested that we pick them up on the way. It was obvious Auntie Jen was not going to make this easy, so Aunt Terri did everything she could to make things as simple as possible. After a little negotiating they agreed to eat lunch at Wilbur's BBQ, which was Big Willie's favorite restaurant. Aunt Terri, and I picked Queenie and Big Willie up at Auntie Jen's house and headed to eat. There was an awkward silence in the car on the way because they did not know Aunt Terri, and they barely knew me. I think they agreed to come for the free meal and so they could get away from Auntie Jen for a little while. I tried to open the conversation, but was shut down quickly, "Hi guys, how's it going?" "Shut up! You're such a little nerd," Queenie said. "Don't talk to her like that," Big Willie chimed in. "You shut up, too. I'll talk to her any way I want to. She ain't nobody," Queenie continued. I could tell Aunt Terri was getting aggravated, and I didn't want her to cancel the whole thing, so I decided to turn on the radio, which made everyone happy.

When we arrived at the restaurant we were seated, and the waitress took our orders. At the table we just sat there in silence until Aunt Terri asked how things were going for them. They looked at each other as if to see if they would tell the truth. Big Willie spoke first, "We're doing ok. I've been worried about mom, and Auntie Jen won't let us go see her. I don't have her address so I can't write her, and I don't know what to do," he confessed. Big Willie was always very quiet and reserved so for him to speak up like this meant he was desperate for help. Queenie was also worried, "Why won't they let us see her?" she cried. I knew it must be very hard on Queenie because they were so close. I felt bad for them, but I had no desire to see the woman who tried to kill me.

Aunt Terri said, "Maybe I can help. I can speak with a lawyer friend of mine who may be able to get visitation, but I am not making any promises. After all, she did try to murder her own child. The court may see her as a danger to you." "My mother has never been a danger to me or my brother. There are only 2 people she hated; one is dead and the other is the reason she is in jail right now. She would never harm a hair on my head," Queenie protested. "Don't sit here and say that in front of Zora. It's not her fault that mom hates her; she's just a little girl. I mean what kind of mother hates her own child?" Big Willie proclaimed. I never knew it, but apparently Big Willie had plenty of opinions about what was happening, but he just never said anything.

"Alright, guys, enough of that kind of talk. We brought you here so you could bond, not talk bad about each other and get into arguments," Aunt Terri declared. I could tell she was upset with Queenie, but she kept her cool. "Now Queenie, how are you dealing with your new living arrangements? You will be starting school soon, and this is your last year, isn't it?" Aunt Terri asked. "Yeah, I will be the only senior with her mother in jail. What a great way to start the year off," Queenie replied sarcastically. "Do you have any plans after high school?" Aunt Terri inquired. "Oh yes, I'm going to Harvard!" Queenie kept on. Aunt Terri had had enough of Queenie's lip and started to let her have it. "Listen young lady, you need to get your head out of your ass and stop blaming the wrong person for what has happened; furthermore, pity parties are not very attractive! You need to grow up and act more mature. Nobody is going to want to help you with that attitude of yours." That must have taken Queenie off guard because she gasped and looked shocked that someone was talking to her in that manner. She was a spoiled brat, and nobody had even raised their voice at her before now. Big Willie seemed to get a kick out of it because he was chuckling to himself.

"Look, lady." Before she could finish her sentence, Aunt Terri interrupted her, "Little girl, don't you ever think you can sass me. If you can't be nice, then sit there and eat your food in silence. I don't know what's wrong with kids these days, but I know one thing they won't be talking to me any kind of way." Aunt Terri was talking to no one in particular. I tried to change the subject by talking to Big Willie, "Are you going out for the varsity team this year?" I knew that had him because his face lit up. "Yeah, I'm pretty excited, but I heard the basketball coach is mean." I had heard tales about this coach also, but I didn't want to scare Big Willie off. "You should be fine. You practice basketball day and night. There's nobody that can play better than you at The Center, and everyone loves you. He won't be mean to you unless you give him a reason," I said. "Maybe you can come watch me play if I make the team. It's been a while since you've seen me play and it might be cool," he replied. "Of course I will. Playing on the varsity squad will be great for you! Daddy always said you would be good." Big Willie just smiled, and he looked very pleased with himself. I wonder if Auntie Jen would allow him to play, but I never said a word to him. I didn't want to start another fight. Meanwhile, Queenie was sitting there quietly eating her food and rolling her eyes at Aunt Terri when she wasn't looking. I could tell nothing would be resolved between the two of us today so I did not push my luck.

After lunch we decided to drive to this gas station up the highway a bit for some ice cream. They had the best hand-dipped ice cream around. I always got a double scoop of butter pecan on a cone, Big Willie loved rocky road, and Queenie always got cherry cheesecake. Aunt Terri decided she would splurge and get some plain old vanilla. "Out of all the flavors, you chose vanilla?" I asked. Aunt Terri laughed and explained that she never really liked any other flavor except vanilla. I couldn't believe my ears. Vanilla was so boring, and Aunt Terri was so exciting and cool. I guess she can't be cool all of the time.

On the way to take Queenie and Big Willie back to Aunty Jen's house, the car got very quiet. Big Willie was in the front seat because he called shotgun at the gas station. I was not happy about it, but I did not complain. I hated sitting in the back seat with Queenie. She always seemed to be in the worst mood and always took it out on me. Today was no exception. "You know I can't stand your ass, don't you?" she started. I tried to ignore her, but she was not having any of that. Before I knew what had happened, Queenie smacked me across the face and punched me in the stomach. She was angry, and I was her target. Automatically my fight instinct kicked in and I punched her in the eye. She pulled my hair, and I got her in a headlock. Aunt Terri was yelling for us to stop, but we did not care. I punched her in the mouth, and she scratched my face. That was the last straw because nobody touches my face and lives. I jumped on top of her and was punching like Sugar Ray Leonard. She couldn't see and had nowhere to go. All hell was breaking loose in that back seat, and Big Willie was getting a kick out of it. Aunt Terri finally pulled over on the side of the road and broke us apart. She had some paper towels in the car, and she made us clean ourselves up as best we could. There was nothing left to say, and neither of us wanted to hear it anyway. "Big Willie will you please switch seats with Queenie so they will not fight anymore?" Aunt Terri asked.

I was fine sitting in the back with Big Willie, and we continued on to Auntie Jen's house. I was hoppin' mad, but I tried to control myself. I couldn't believe that tramp actually scratched my face. When she got out of the car I was planning to trip her and make her fall flat on her face. Seeing that would make the beating I would get later worth it. Unfortunately, Aunt Terri knew what I was plotting and forced me to stay in the car until Queenie was out of my sight. Auntie Jen tried to act a fool when she saw Queenie's face, but Aunt Terri stopped her dead in her tracks "Jen, don't mess with me! These damn kids have worked my last nerve, and I am not in the mood. This one (Queenie) decided to beat up her little sister, but couldn't handle the fire power. This one (me) decided she was not going to be a punching bag and lit into her before I could pull over. Believe me Zora will get her tail torn when we get home. I'm sorry this happened, but it is not something I plan on discussing any further."

I knew I was in for it when I got home, but I didn't care. I was sick and tired of being picked on by Queenie, and I wasn't going to let her think she could beat me up anytime she wanted. Aunt Terri said to me as soon as we walked in the front door, "What do you want for dinner?" "Huh," was all I could manage to say. "Use proper English when responding to me, young lady. Again, what do you want for dinner?" She winked at me and gave me a huge smile which let me know I was off the hook. "Can we have pizza?" I asked. "We sure can," replied Aunt Terri. "Now get upstairs and clean yourself up before your uncle gets home. I do not plan on punishing you for defending yourself, but you will have to tell your uncle. He may or may not punish you," Aunt Terri declared.

When Uncle Jim came home from work, he was dog tired and was not in the mood for my drama. During dinner he asked how my day went, and that was my opening to tell him. I told Uncle Jim in great detail what happened, and he said, "If that girl touches you again, make sure you knock her head off." That was all he said, and I was relieved. Later Aunt Terri explained the reason I wasn't punished was because I was defending myself. She also made it clear under no uncertain terms was I to initiate any violence against anyone, especially my sister. She said I should focus on trying to mend fences and sticking together during a time like this. Aunt Terri said, "Just think how hard it must be for Queenie. Her best friend and the one person in the world on who she could depend is in jail for trying to kill her daughter. Queenie must be torn between loving you and being loyal to her mom. The father she longed for most of her life is dead and both instances involve you. She has to know deep down that it's not your fault, but she can't say that because she doesn't want to betray her mom and dad." I never looked at it from her point of view before, and now that Aunt Terri pointed it out, I felt bad. I wanted to do something to help both her and Big Willie. I had Aunt Terri and Uncle Jim to take care of me, and they loved me more and more every day. They only had Auntie Jen, and it was evident that she did not want them around.

Since summer was coming to an end fast, and school would be starting soon, I asked Aunt Terri if we could use some of the money that Daddy left me to take Queenie and Big Willie school shopping. I know that Queenie was used to having all of the great clothes, and this year was her senior year. It would mean a lot to her if she could still be one of the best dressed girls at school. Big Willie needed new sneakers so he could make the basketball team, and he always liked to look good for the ladies. Aunt Terri agreed that it would be a good thing to do, but also warned me not to get used to using money to bond with my siblings. She said sometimes people substitute love for money, and that always turns out badly. I think this one time it would be nice for my sister and brother to have a little normalcy in their life. They were so used to getting what they wanted before Mr. Samuels came into our lives, and I wanted them to feel happy even if it was temporary.

Chapter 18: Shopping for Drama

In order to complete my request about school shopping for my siblings, Aunt Terri had to get approval from Vivi since she was in charge of the money. We made an appointment to meet at her office and went to see her. Vivi was always happy to see me, and this time was no exception. "Hi Miss Zora. It's good to see you!" Vivi said while giving me a big hug. "What brings you to my office?" she asked. "Hi Vivi, I miss you, and I have some money stuff I need to ask you about. Aunt Terri said we should make an appointment instead of calling," I replied. "Well come right in and have a seat, ladies," Vivi said with enthusiasm. I thought about what I would say to Vivi all night. I wanted her to approve my request so I could help my brother and sister just a little.

"Vivi, I would like to have some money to purchase back-to-school clothes for Big Willie and Queenie," I said with confidence. Vivi's face twisted, and then she said, "Zora, I want you to really think about this. It could be the start of something you can't finish. I don't want your family to think that every time they need something they can ask you for money. It would be giving them the wrong impression, and I do not intend to let you support your siblings with your trust money. Your father left you that money so you could go to college and be taken care of for the rest of your days. It is not to support others in your family. He specifically stated in his will that this was not his goal for this money. He wanted to protect you from your mother and her love for money." "I understand all of that, Vivi, and I had a big talk with Aunt Terri before making this appointment. I will make it very clear to my siblings that this is a one-time only deal, and I will not be able to help them with every little thing. I just want Queenie to have a good senior year, and Big Willie wants to play varsity basketball, and he will need shoes and new gear. With Teresa Langston in jail they don't have any money right now. I'm sure Auntie Jen will be able to help them going forward, but right now I want to. Each one of them has saved my life, and I owe them. Just this once." I made my case and waited for Vivi to respond, but instead she asked me to leave the room so she could speak with Aunt Terri alone. I was not happy about that because it was technically my money, and I did not want to be left out of conversations about it.

"Vivi and Aunt Terri, I don't think it's right for me to leave the room so you can talk about me and my money. I have a right to be in the room," I proclaimed. This must have taken them both by surprise because they looked at me as if I had lost my mind. "Zora, I asked politely the first time. I will not be so nice the second time and if I have to say it three times, there will be a big problem." Vivi meant business, so I quickly got up and went to the lobby to wait for Aunt Terri. I don't know what they were talking about, but I was sure the answer would be no. As I sat in the lobby, I thought of ways to convince Vivi to give me the money. I hated not being in control, and I really hated being told no. It wasn't fair that I had money but could not use it to help my family. It wasn't their fault that our mother was crazy and tried to kill me. They had been punished enough by losing their crazy, child molesting father and now their murderous mother.

When Aunt Terri called me back into Vivi's office I was told that Vivi decided to approve the withdrawal this one time, but she would not do so again. I had to make sure to inform Queenie and Big Willie that they would not be able to obtain any more money from my trust fund ever again. Aunt Terri said she would make that part easy because she and Uncle Jim would be present when we went shopping, and they would make it clear.

I couldn't wait to get home and call Big Willie. I decided I would talk to him first and let him reveal the news to Queenie. It took some doing, but I was able to convince Big Willie that what I was doing was not charity. I told him how I felt bad about what happened to them and wanted to at least take some pressure off by buying clothes for the school year. It took me promising to buy a pair of Converse All Stars before he agreed. All of the upper classmen were wearing them, and it would make Big Willie look super cool. He was tickled to be getting a pair of "Chuck Taylors," but he did not let it show on the outside. Big Willie had a really smooth way of convincing people to do things, and he was able to get Queenie to agree to the shopping spree by appealing to her fashion sense. He told her about overhearing one of her former friends talking about the clothes she was getting this year for school. Willie knew Queenie could not be outdone by her arch enemy. They were both on board, and my plan was working great, except one thing. Auntie Jen wanted something, too. She was trying to get anything she could out of me by asking for a reward for taking care of my brother and sister. Aunt Terri and Vivi put a stop to that right away.

"Jen, you will not be participating in the back-to-school shopping. This is a one-time deal that was approved by the trustee. The purpose is to purchase school clothes for Zora's siblings only, and that does not include you. Besides it's been a very long time since you graced the hallways of any school," Vivi informed Auntie Jen. Apparently the two of them had a past. They were high school classmates until Auntie Jen dropped out. Vivi disliked Auntie Jen because she had stolen Vivi's boyfriend when they were in the 10th grade. Vivi never forgave her and was holding a grudge all this time. Vivi said the bad thing about it was Auntie Jen never even liked the boy; she just wanted to see if she could steal him away.

Our shopping trip started out fun. Queenie and Big Willie seemed excited to go out and get whatever they wanted for school. Aunt Terri agreed to buy not only clothes, but also school supplies. Instead of the regular old stores we went to in Goldsboro, Aunt Terri drove us to Raleigh to Crabtree Valley Mall. She decided we should make a day of it, and since it was Saturday, Uncle Jim was able to go, too. Vivi decided she would pass on the shopping because she was not into it. Uncle Jim told me how proud he was that I was thinking of someone other than myself. That meant the world to me. He said there was something Godly in the way I forgave Queenie for her mistreatment of me, and he admired that. I didn't know anything about being Godly, all I knew was she was still my sister, and I wanted her to love me. Plus she saved me from drowning at the pool that day. I was just happy to still be around.

Our road trip to Raleigh was fun because we played music and sang. Both Queenie and Big Willie were in good moods and helped us sing the songs. We had never had a day like this before, and I was enjoying it. All that began to change once we actually started shopping. Queenie was trying on clothes and asked that I help her in the dressing room. I thought this was odd, but I was hoping that maybe this would be a bonding experience for the both of us. Boy, was I wrong! As soon as we entered the dressing room Queenie showed her true colors, as the old people would say.

"Zora, I don't need any help trying on clothes. I wanted to talk to you about something," she said in a hushed tone. "What is it Queenie?" I replied. "Well, I went to see Mommy the other day, and she needs your help." My heart dropped to my stomach, and I began to feel queasy. What kind of help could I possibly be to the woman who tried to drown me? I felt uncomfortable talking about this with Queenie, and Aunt Terri had already warned me not to discuss this with anyone because the trial was coming up soon. "What kind of help?" I asked. "You see, Zora, if you will say that she was trying to save you in the pool instead of saying she was trying to hurt you, her lawyer may be able to get the charges dropped, and she won't have to stay in jail. I really need you to do this favor for me," she said with desperation in her voice. "Queenie, I would like to help you, but I can't lie to the court. I could get in big trouble. Besides, there were about 30 other people there who saw what happened. I can't lie for them, too," I answered. I really did want to help Queenie, but I had no intention of getting Teresa Langston out of jail. "Mommy's lawyer said if you take back what you said, it would go better for her. You can be the one to save her. Don't you want to save Mommy?" She must have been out of her mind! Why in heaven's name would I want to save the very woman who tried to kill me? She has hated me since I was born and never loved me or my daddy. I knew what this was. I must be on that Candid Camera TV Show. I started laughing and looking around the dressing room for cameras, but I did not find any. "What are you doing?" she asked. "I'm looking for cameras. This is a joke, right? Some man with a camera is going to pop out and say gotcha! Am I right?" I replied.

"No, bitch, this ain't a joke. My mom and yours is locked up in jail and has no way of getting out unless you lie and say she did not try to hurt you. You need to do this so I can get out of Auntie Jen's house. You don't know what it's like to live with her. She is mean to me and treats me bad because I am pretty and she is getting older. It's not my fault her boyfriends seem to like me better than her. I can't stay in a house where someone hates me. "Oh, you mean like you and your mom treated me? Welcome to my world! I never had a day of peace when I lived with you all. Daddy was the only person who kept you off of me, and when he died you both acted like he never mattered.

That was hurtful! I needed you as a big sister, and you hated me just for being born. You have been nasty to me all of my life, and now I'm supposed to feel sorry for your mom, the very same witch who tried to kill me? Are you out of your cotton pickin' mind? I will never- you hear me- never lie to get her out of jail. They need to bury her under the jail. She not only deserves to be punished, she needs it. How else will she learn that she can't go around trying to kill people? Not just random people, her own flesh and blood!" By this time I was yelling at the top of my lungs, and I had started crying, too. Aunt Terri heard the commotion and burst into the dressing room just as Queenie was punching me in the face. My lip started bleeding, and I was in a rage. How dare she act like this was my fault after everything I had to put up with? All of the hurt and pain I had in me decided to come out all at once and I went crazy. I jumped on Queenie and started wailing on her. Before Aunt Terri and Uncle Jim could pull us apart, I had done considerable damage. I didn't know what came over me. All I knew was I felt rage like I had never felt before. Queenie was shocked and looked scared and confused all at the same time.

"Zora, apologize to your sister right now!" Aunt Terri demanded. "No!" I shouted. "Girl, don't back talk me. Now I said apologize to her," she repeated. "Aunt Terri, I love you, but I will never apologize to this tramp for what I did. She needs to apologize to me for asking me to lie to get her mom out of jail. She has always thought my feelings don't matter. Well, those days are over, you hear me, over! People are gonna know how I feel from now on, and they are gonna respect me!" I shouted. I pushed past Uncle Jim and left the dressing room. I stormed past the shocked sales ladies and the customers and found myself walking through the mall. I had to get out of there before I really hurt someone. By this time I was afraid of myself, and I did not like that feeling. I never wanted to feel this way again. I was out of control, and all I knew to do was get away from Queenie before I killed her. I walked and walked and cried the whole time. When I finally stopped, I was at the end of the mall where the little kids went to play and ride on the train. I sat on a bench, and when I saw my reflection in a store window, I saw how crazy I looked. My eyes were bloodshot from crying, and I had tear stains on my face. My hair was sticking up all over my head because of the fight, and my shirt was hanging off of me. People were staring at me like I was crazy, and one lady came over to see if I needed any help.

"Sweetie, are you ok?" she said. "Yes ma'am. I am fine. I just got into a tussle with my sister. I didn't mean to scare the kids. I will leave now," I replied. "No sweetie, don't leave. Just get yourself together. Are your parents looking for you? They must be." "No ma'am, my daddy is dead, and I don't have a mom. I am here with my aunt and uncle. They will know where to find me. I will be fine. I just need to splash some water on my face. Thank you." I did not have the strength to explain to a total stranger that my mom tried to kill me, and my sister wanted her out of jail. I felt like I needed to run away from this lady, but I kept it together. Just then I saw the ladies restroom, and I excused myself. I went into the last stall and just sat there. Before I knew what happened, I was crying and wailing. I got so worked up that I made myself sick and had to throw up. I didn't know what to do, and I became scared. I wanted my daddy, and he couldn't come to rescue me. What was I going to do? I had disobeyed Aunt Terri, I fought with my sister, and now I was sitting in this lonely bathroom by myself vomiting into the toilet. I needed help, so I started praying. Grandma Rose always told me to pray when I felt lost, and God would be there to comfort me. Through all of my heartache and pain I had never felt like giving up before, and I was close to it now. "Please God, help me. I don't know what to do," I started praying out loud. Just then there was a knock on the stall door. "Sweetie, are you alright?" It was the nice lady from the benches. She had followed me into the bathroom. God must have sent her to help me. "Yes ma'am, I just feel a little sick. Can you please go to Customer Service and have them page my uncle?" "Of course, but wouldn't you rather have your Aunt since you are in the ladies?" "No I need my uncle. He will know how to help me," I said.

"What's his name sweetie?" "His name is Jim Langston," I managed to get out before getting sick again. "I'll be right back. You stay right there."

The lady left the bathroom and a few minutes later I heard a man's voice come over the intercom paging Uncle Jim to the Customer Service Desk. A few minutes later Uncle Jim burst into the ladies restroom in a panic. "Babygirl, are you in here?" He was out of breath like he had been running, and he sounded scared. "I'm in here," I said faintly from the bathroom stall. I unlocked the door, and he came in. The nice lady from the bench was there as was security. Everyone looked so concerned that I must have been a sight. "Babygirl, what is going on? Are you alright?" Uncle Jim wanted to know. "I don't feel very well, and I have been throwing up. I'm scared, Uncle Jim" I said through my tears. "Come now, you will be alright. I think you are making yourself sick with all this stress. Come on out here and wash your face, and let's get you fixed up." Uncle Jim asked everyone to leave and waited while I washed my face and fixed my clothes. He also helped me put my hair in a ponytail so I wouldn't look like I lived in the wild. As I was leaving the bathroom, there was a crowd of people waiting and watching. I was so embarrassed, but Uncle Jim told me to keep my head held high and walk with pride. He said everyone has a meltdown every now and then, but you have to bounce back and show the world you are still here and ready for your next challenge.

The car was silent on the way home, and I sat up front with Uncle Jim and Aunt Terri to avoid any further issues. Queenie was beat up, but she did not look too bad. Big Willie sat in the back next to her, but ignored her most of the ride. He was happy to get his Converse and new clothes and told her how stupid she had been to cause such a scene. She did not even get any school clothes because of her scheme. I decided then and there I would much rather hang out with boys. Girls bring too much drama for me. They just did not get me. So much for my brilliant idea…

121

Chapter 19: Zora's Head Gets Shrunk

After the incident in the mall, Aunt Terri was very concerned about my well- being. She wanted to sit down with me, Uncle Jim, and Vivi to discuss what happened and to see what if anything she could do to help the situation. I explained to her why I was upset, but I don't think she really understood my point of view. This made me even more upset, and I just stopped talking. It wasn't doing me any good to talk. It seemed like the more I talked, the more confused she became. Finally Uncle Jim said, "Terri, leave that poor girl alone. She has been through enough, and she doesn't need to feel like she is being badgered in her own home; enough already." But that wasn't enough for Aunt Terri "Well, if she won't talk to me, then she will have to go see a professional. There is something wrong with her, and I am going to get to the bottom of this." This angered me. "There isn't anything wrong with me! The problem is nobody understands me or the way I feel. When I try to express myself, you get even more upset. so I stop. That doesn't sound like some cuckoo crazy girl! I am NOT crazy, and I don't want my head shrunk." I did not know of a way to make it any clearer, and I did not have the patience to try. "You see what I'm saying? She keeps having these outbursts, and they are getting more and more violent. Did you see what she did to her sister?" Uncle Jim said, "Terri, honey, didn't you tell me that Queenie punched her in the mouth as you were opening the door to the dressing room? Babygirl was just taking up for herself. I don't think she needs to see a shrink for that." "Listen, you brought me here to help take care of this little girl. She is my responsibility, and I know something is wrong. You can't possibly go through all of the tragedy that she has faced and not need help. It's just not humanly possible. Nobody is saying she's crazy, but she needs a better way to let those feeling out or she is going to explode. I have the final word, and she's going!"

There was nothing left to say. Once Aunt Terri dug her heels in, there was no reasoning with her. Her mind was made up and that was the way it was going to be. I couldn't fight Aunt Terri anymore, so I gave in. Aunt Terri had already made the appointment, and I was scheduled to go on Tuesday morning at 10. Since it was Sunday, I had two days to come up with a plan to keep my head intact. I had no intention of telling some stranger all of my business, and I was not going to give Aunt Terri the satisfaction of being right. I knew I was not crazy, and I was going to make sure everyone else knew it, too. For the next two days I moped around the house and would not even look at Aunt Terri. I tried to stay in my room, but she kept coming in there to check on me. I did everything I could not to speak to her and only did so if I knew I would get in trouble if I did not. I isolated myself and decided I could not trust anyone anymore. Aunt Terri had turned Uncle Jim and Vivi against me, and I was angry about it. Well I decided that she could send me to the shrink, but I didn't have to talk to her. If she wanted to waste my trust money on a doctor I didn't need, fine, but I was not going to help her lock me up in the nuthouse. I saw *One Flew Over the Cuckoo's Nest* when I was younger, and that place is not for me. If she thought she was locking me away in there with that mean Nurse Ratched, she had another thought coming. I would sneak out in the middle of the night, and they would never see me again.

On Tuesday I got up got dressed and was waiting in the living room for Aunt Terri to take me to the doctor's office. I was still salty and did not speak to her when she said good morning. That must have pissed her off because she began yelling at me. "I have had enough of your foolishness, Zora. I expect to receive a greeting when I speak to you. You may not like what I am doing, but I still demand respect. You have been quite disrespectful the last couple of days, and I will not tolerate it anymore! When you get back from your appointment, we are going to have a nice long talk, young lady." I did not care what she said, I still was not going to talk to her, and she couldn't force me.

When we arrived at the therapist's office, it was different than I imagined. I thought it would look like the one in the movie, but it was very bright and cheerful. As I entered the office I saw toys and a table like they had in school for us to do arts and crafts on one side. On the other side was a desk with pictures in frames and lots of books on shelves. There were framed diplomas on the wall and on one side, a very cushy couch. The office was very big, and there were other chairs arranged around the room so the doctor could talk to several people at one time. My head was full of questions that I dared not ask out loud. What if this doctor decided I was crazy? What if Uncle Jim let Aunt Terri lock me up in the nuthouse? Would I spend the rest of my life looking out the window wishing I could have fresh air and wanting to get away from the crazy people? Where did they keep the machine that would shrink my head? I guessed I would find out soon enough.

As my mind was wandering, I heard the office door open. In walked the lady from the benches at the mall. She was smiling and looked happy to see me. What was she doing here? Then I saw Uncle Jim and Vivi walk in behind her. I felt like passing out, and in my head I kept thinking that they were all here to lock me away! I felt panicky and wanted to run, but I made myself stay put. I would never forgive Aunt Terri for this. She had turned everyone I had left in this world against me and I was beginning to hate her. She was no better than Teresa Langston in my eyes. First she pretended to love me, and now that things were a little rocky, she wanted to get rid of me. At least with Teresa Langston I never had to wonder: she always hated me. Thinking that you are loved and then finding out it was a lie was worse than being hated up front. I wanted to leave, but I knew they would have me arrested, and the police would put me in the Cuckoo's Nest. Then I remembered something Grandma Rose used to say, "If God be for you, who can be against you?" I played those words over and over in my head, and I gained confidence. I decided to defy them. I was not going to let anyone lock me away, and God would protect me from them like He always did.

It turned out the lady from the benches was the doctor! That must have been how Aunt Terri got an appointment so quickly. She must have made it on Saturday at the mall. Uncle Jim looked at me and then looked down at the ground like he was guilty. This scared me a little because Uncle Jim never looked down, and he always said to look people square in the eye when dealing with them. "Hey Babygirl, it's good to see you. I missed you at breakfast this morning because I had to get to work early so I could be here. Vivi and I came for moral support and to make things easier on your first day of therapy," he said while looking at his shoes. I did not say a word; I just stared at him until he was so uncomfortable that he wanted a glass of water. He thought it would be easier for me to have my head put in one of those machines to shrink it if he was here? He must have been crazy, too. Vivi never said a word, but I could feel her eyes burning my skin. I looked her straight in the eyes, and she looked away also. I knew I was in big trouble now, because Vivi wasn't afraid of anyone, and she never backed down from a challenge. She actually looked away from me which to me meant she was either afraid or hiding something.

Either way I was not pleased.

The doctor began talking first and tried to be all nice and sweet, grinning in my face. I looked at her as if she was crazy. I had a good mind to use some of the words I learned from the older kids at the movies, but I decided I would wait to see how things played out. I knew their plan: first they would butter me up being really nice, then once they saw that didn't work they would get more aggressive, and finally they would tie me down on a table and put those things on my head and shrink it. I remembered that movie very well because it scared me. Now I had to be smarter than them. I'd go along with their nice treatment so they wouldn't get too upset. I would say things they wanted to hear and this should make them think I was normal. Yeah, that's what I would do, and they would be forced to leave me alone once this doctor told them I was not crazy. I was going to beat them at their own game. Once I was declared normal I would trick Vivi into giving me some money, and I would run away and join the circus. That way everyone would have what they wanted; Aunt Terri could have Uncle Jim all to herself again: Vivi would still have her law office, and I would have my freedom.

"Good morning, Zora. Do you remember me from the mall? My name is Dr. Boggs, and I want you to make yourself at home," she started in. "Good morning, and yes, I remember you. Thank you for helping me the other day. I never got a chance to thank you properly," I replied with a slight grin. I could feel everyone's eyes on me waiting to see how I would react to the doctor. I decided it was time to get my Academy Award. I was going to give the performance of my life and set myself free! "Zora, we are here today because there was some concern that you need help expressing yourself. I was told about some of the things that have happened to you, and I would like us to explore how you are feeling about them, okay?" Her sugary sweet manner was making me sick and I felt like throwing up, but instead I smiled sweetly and said, "Okay, Dr. Boggs." She wanted me to start by telling her what happened at the mall to trigger the fight with my sister. She was being so careful not to blame me, and I saw right through it. Here was my chance to see if I could be the writer I wanted to be when I grew up. I would tell her just a little and make her want more and more of my story. Then I would hit her with the real stuff and knock her socks off. "What caused you to get so angry with your sister in the dressing room?" she continued. "She hit me," I said. "And why would she do that? Weren't you having a good time shopping for school clothes? Why would she just hit you out of nowhere? What did you say to her right before she hit you?" the doctor asked. These questions made my blood boil. It was as if she was saying it was all my fault just like Aunt Terri. People never understood me, and now I was being blamed because my selfish sister decided to hit me, and I reacted. This taught me a big lesson: the first person to hit never gets caught, and it's always the one who hits back who is blamed. I knew why I was here now; they wanted me to say it was my fault. Aunt Terri wanted me to apologize to Queenie, and I would never do that. "I told her no," I replied.

"I find it hard to believe that a reasonable person would hit another person just because they said no. There must be more to the story that you are leaving out," continued this quack of a doctor. I couldn't believe my ears; this lady already blamed me twice, and she didn't even ask the real question, like what did she ask you to do? Nobody cared about that.

"Well, that's what happened," I said dryly "Tell me this, why did you pummel her?

"I did what any normal person would do. I reacted to violence with violence. I know God said turn the other cheek, but in this instance I had no more cheeks left. What do you do when a person hurts you so much so that you have no cheeks left? I'll tell you what you do, you defend yourself, and that's what I did."

I was getting angry now, and my little plan was about to go out of the window. If she asked me just one more stupid question, I would blast her! Wait a minute, that's what she was trying to do. She wanted me to get angry just like Aunt Terri told her I did. She was using these questions to make me react. She was throwing the first punch, so I had to control my actions and outsmart her.

"From the description of your sister's face, it sounds like you did more than just defend yourself, and why didn't you apologize when your aunt asked you to?" she chided. "My lip was bleeding, and the only thing I heard was: "Zora, apologize to your sister." That was wrong. Aunt Terri saw her hit me first, but I was told to apologize and take the blame. She never even asked what happened, so I got upset and ran away. No big deal. It won't happen again because I know better now," I said calmly. I could tell this was not the reaction everyone expected because they were all looking at me with shocked expressions; everyone except Uncle Jim. He constantly looked down at the floor and would only look up every now and then. Could he be feeling guilty for making me come here? I wondered, if I got him on my side, maybe we wouldn't have to come back.

"Well our time is almost up for today. I would like to see you at least three times a week until I can get a better fix on things. I want you to take this journal and write in it every time you feel angry or if you feel you are being treated unfairly. From now on, we will meet one-on-one so you can feel more comfortable expressing yourself. I have an opening tomorrow at 10; will that fit your schedule, Terri?" she asked. "Yes, doctor, I'll make sure she is here on time," Aunt Terri replied. "Great, and I will see you tomorrow, Miss Zora." I smiled sweetly and said goodbye to the doctor, and that is just what I meant. I wasn't coming back to this quack. Couldn't Aunt Terri see this lady was milking them for the money? We didn't even talk about anything. All she did was accuse me and try to provoke me, and it didn't work.

Vivi said goodbye, but she did not hug me like she usually did, so I asked her why. "Vivi, why didn't I get a hug?" I said partly trying to provoke her with my newly learned skills.

"Because I don't hug little girls who act disrespectfully towards their aunt and uncle. You know better than to test me, Zora, but walking around not speaking to your aunt is just plain mean and hurtful. I do not intend to hug you again until the Zora I know returns," she said drily. "Well I guess our days of hugging are over," I said smartly as I walked away. As I got into the car I could hear Vivi going off in the background. I felt bad for sassing her, but she was scheming to lock me up, and I wasn't going to pretend like everything was peaches and cream. I wanted her to know that I was hurting too, but my smart mouth just made her angry. I couldn't wait to get home so I could go to my room and read. I needed the solitude of a good book and to get away from people that no longer liked me.

As soon as we walked into the house I attempted to go to my room, but Aunt Terri had other plans. "Where do you think you're going?" she asked. "To my room," I replied. "Did you conveniently forget that we need to have a talk? Get your behind back down those stairs and sit on this couch," she demanded. I was usually afraid of Aunt Terri's stern voice and did whatever she said, but this time I wasn't scared. I would go along with her authority for now, but I would let her know that she couldn't boss me around like a puppy. I came back downstairs, but instead of sitting on the couch, I sat in Uncle Jim's favorite recliner, kicked back, and put my feet up. I knew this would annoy Aunt Terri, and that was my goal. "Oh hell no, you have lost your damn mind. Girl you better get your butt up and sit where I told you to sit. What is your problem, Zora?" "You, you're my problem; ever since you blamed me for that incident in the mall with Queenie!" I yelled. That seemed to throw Aunt Terri off-guard. "What do you mean?" she asked. "I didn't blame you for anything!"

"Oh yes you did. I know you were listening outside the dressing room because I saw your feet. You heard everything she said to me, and then you stood right there and watched her hit me. When I got mad and hit her back you yelled at me and told me to apologize to her. I couldn't believe it! You turned on me just like everyone else. I thought I could trust you." By this time I wanted to cry. I did not want Aunt Terri to see me cry. She was the enemy now, and I could not show weakness around her, so I sucked it up.

"Zora, I never took her side. I just wanted you to apologize because I knew she never would. You were supposed to be the bigger person, but you let your anger control you. I wasn't taking her side, and I did not blame you. Your sister is having a hard time, and she needed to be right," she explained.

"Well, I have needed someone on my side since my daddy died, and I thought you were that person. Queenie and her mom always treated me like a piece of dirt on their clean floor. Never once have they ever been nice to me, and the one time my sister is nice, it turns out she wanted something. Yes, she saved me from drowning, but I don't think she knew what she was doing. It was instinct; if she had thought about who she was saving she would have let me drown. I know that now. I don't want anything to do with her again, and for you to tell me to apologize was the ultimate betrayal. You're my aunt, not hers. You should always take up for me no matter what, but you didn't. And now you've turned Uncle Jim and Vivi against me. I don't have anyone!" I broke down crying and couldn't control myself. I didn't care anymore about enemies and playing stupid games. All I wanted was to have things go back to how they were before the trip to the mall. Aunt Terri came over and held me. She held me so tightly I thought I would suffocate, but I did not care. I needed her to hold me and tell me things would be alright, and she did.

Chapter 20: Beach Therapy

When Uncle Jim arrived home I could tell he was still bothered by the therapy session. He still would not look at me, and he did not want to look at Aunt Terri. He looked tired and worn down and said, "Terri, we need to talk. Now I went along with this therapy thing because you said it would help Babygirl, but I just don't see it. That doctor did nothing to help her. All she did was accuse her of hurting Queenie and blame her for what happened. From what I saw, Zora was defending herself, and I would tell her to do it again. I don't want Babygirl going back to that place, and that's it. I have the last say as the man of the house, and I don't want any lip about it."

It seemed like Uncle Jim had thought long and hard about this all day, and he finally found the right way to say it. Too bad it took him so long because Aunt Terri and I had already decided therapy wasn't for me. We had spent the rest of the day discussing what happened and making up. Apparently there wasn't really a room where they shrink your head in a machine. Aunt Terri said people in an asylum were subjected to electro shock therapy as a last resort, and that she would never lock me away in there. We were waiting for dinner to break the news to Uncle Jim, but he beat us to the punch.

"Ok Jim, whatever you think is right," Aunt Terri replied as she winked at me. It was to be our little secret, or so we thought. "What, no lip? What is going on, Terri?" Uncle Jim asked. He was looking at Aunt Terri like she was up to something, and he knew it. She had no choice but to tell him about our conversation earlier in the day. "Well Jim, Zora and I had a long talk this afternoon, and we concluded that she does not need therapy right now. We think the best thing for her would be to continue the open door policy we have, and I promised that we will listen going forward," she confessed. "You women think you are slick. Here I was worrying about this all day long and come home to hear it has already been resolved. You could have at least called me at work," he replied. "Baby, I didn't want to bother you at work, plus I had no idea it was worrying you so much. Otherwise I would have called you," Aunt Terri answered. "Well, you two may have had your say, but I still need to clear some things up with Babygirl. I don't like how all this went down, and I need to get this out." Uncle Jim was very serious, and he still looked very sad. I wondered if he really thought I was crazy.

"Uncle Jim, we made your favorite dinner," I said trying to change the subject. I had talked all day with Aunt Terri, and to be honest I was tired of talking. All I wanted to do was eat, watch a little TV, and go to bed. I didn't even want to read tonight which was weird for me. "Babygirl, stop trying to change the subject. We can sit down to dinner after I wash up, and then I am going to have my say." He walked out of the kitchen and went to wash up for dinner. Aunt Terri and I shrugged our shoulders at each other and got dinner on the table. After saying the blessing, Uncle Jim started right in. "Babygirl, I want you to know that I never wanted to send you to that doctor. I don't believe in shrinks, and this lady seemed to be trying to make you mad just so she could diagnose you with something. It made me very uncomfortable, and I know you did not like it either. Your Aunt Terri thought maybe this lady could help you with some of you outbursts, but I still say people are supposed to have outbursts. We all have emotions, and when we hold them in they reach a boiling point and then they explode. Babygirl, you have got to find a way to express your feeling in a positive way that will let everything that's bothering you out without hurting anyone. Your Uncle Jim does that through music. I learned as a small child that music was a place that soothes me. You have to have an outlet. I watch you and see how much you love to read, but I never see you write. You have a strong imagination, and I think you could express yourself by writing stories and poems or just by writing down what you are feeling. Don't get me wrong; I'm not trying to tell you what your outlet should be. It's just a suggestion. What do you think?"

Uncle Jim's words danced around in my head, and he was right. I had the journal I won from the summer reading program, but I never opened it to write. I loved to read, but I never thought someone would want to read anything I wrote. Maybe nobody has to read it. I just need to write it. "Uncle Jim, I think that is a wonderful idea! I have all these feelings in my head that I could write down. Sometimes I have lots of thoughts, but I don't know what to do with them. From now on, I will write them down."

I know I have said this before, but this time it felt different. I had to get them out, and I did not want to talk to anyone about what happened to me. It would be like talking to God, and He already knew what happened, so I could talk openly without being judged. Uncle Jim seemed pleased that I was taking his advice and kept on talking. "I've thought about this all day, and I haven't had a chance to discuss it with Aunt Terri, but I want to take you ladies on a small little vacation before the summer ends." When I heard Uncle Jim say that I got so excited. I loved to travel and it would be fun with just the three of us. Nothing ever worked out whenever we invited more people, but when the three of us were together there was no stopping us! "Where are we going?" I said jumping up from my seat. Laughing Uncle Jim said, "I was thinking the beach. You like the sand and the ocean, don't you?" Was he kidding me? I wish I lived at the beach. I couldn't wait to feel the sand squish between my toes and smell that ocean air. I started screaming and jumping up and down; I just couldn't control myself. "Uncle Jim!!! Can we go now?" I screamed.

"Wait a minute, nobody has asked me, and Jim, you know I hate the beach." When Aunt Terri said those words all of the air left the room, and I felt like I was suffocating. What did she mean she hates the beach? She told me earlier that she loved the beach when they lived in California. What had changed? "Just kidding!" Aunt Terri said as she fell out laughing. She thought she was so funny giving me a heart attack like that. Old people always think their jokes are funny, but kids never laugh. I just stood there looking at her like she was crazy. "I guess it wasn't funny to you, huh? Don't be like that, Zora. I was just playing around," Aunt Terri said. I just shook my head and started asking questions. "Uncle Jim, when are we going? How long are we staying? What beach are we going to? Where are we staying? How long will it take to get there? Can I go shopping for a new swimsuit?" I couldn't help it: I had all of these questions, and I was so excited that I could not wait for the answers.

"Well, a friend of mine has a house on the beach down in South Carolina, and he is letting us use it this weekend. You ever heard of Myrtle Beach, Babygirl? Well we are going to be staying a few miles up the road in Atlantic Beach. We can still go up to Myrtle Beach and see all of the sites if you want. We'll leave on Friday after work and come back on Monday. How does that sound?" Uncle Jim said with a smile. "It sounds wonderful," I squealed. "Your friend is so lucky to have a house on the beach! I can't believe it. I'm going to pack right now."

"Hold on a minute. There's plenty of time for that, but right now you need to finish your dinner. Sit down eat and let's get our plan together" Aunt Terri demanded. I did as I was told, but all I could think about was getting to that beach. Imagine having a house where the ocean is your back yard; nothing but sand and surf to spend your days on. This seemed like heaven to me and I couldn't wait to experience it.

The rest of the week I spent dreaming about the ocean. I wanted to learn how to surf like the people on TV. I couldn't wait to build a sandcastle with Uncle Jim, and he promised he was an expert at making them. I wanted to run and jump in the waves until I was too tired to move, then I would lie on a beach towel and take a nap, wake up, and do it all over again. I found myself writing in my journal and trying to draw pictures of the activities I wanted to do. I have never been able to draw, so my pictures did not look like I imagined them in my head. I convinced Aunt Terri to take me shopping to buy new swim suits for the beach. It didn't take much effort because she wanted new gear, too. While we were at the mall, she decided to get Uncle Jim new swim trunks also. "Butterfly, it's the end of the summer, and you know all the swimsuits are on sale! Feel free to get two if you can find some that you like. Right now they are 70% off," Aunt Terri instructed. We were having so much fun shopping that I did not even see Vivi standing there watching us.

"Well guess who made up. I suppose you are acting like a respectable young lady again," she kidded. "Hi Vivi, how are you?" I asked. I thought she may still be mad at me, but at least she was in a good mood. "I am well, Miss Zora. I see your senses have returned," she continued. I was not happy that she kept talking slick, but I chose to ignore it. "Yep and Uncle Jim is taking us to the beach," I beamed. "Well, well, well I guess it's ok for you to act a fool," she continued. "You know Vivi, I had my reasons, but I do not need you to keep bringing it up. Aunt Terri has forgiven me and we have moved on. I wish you would," I said as I walked off to look at sandals. Vivi stood there watching me, her eyes burning a hole in my skin. I had had enough of her lip, and I needed her to know she could not just continue to talk down to me. If she wanted respect from me, she would have to give it. I saw her turn and start talking to Aunt Terri, and then she came over to say goodbye. "I have to get back to the office and wanted to say goodbye. Have fun at the beach," she said.

"Thanks, Vivi. It was good seeing you," I said. It felt like I was talking to a stranger and I did not like that feeling. I walked over and hugged her goodbye, and she smiled. I knew things between us would be fine after that.

Friday finally arrived, and Aunt Terri rushed around to make sure she packed everything for her and Uncle Jim, made a picnic dinner for us to take on the road, and cleaned the house. "Butterfly, make sure you pack everything you need because if you forget anything, we won't be coming back," she warned. "I have everything I need. I packed last night," I answered as I attempted to help her clean. She was rushing around so much that anything I did, she just undid until I finally gave up. When Uncle Jim came home, we hit the road, and I couldn't wait. As usual, Uncle Jim gave us a concert on the way to the beach. He was always so much fun on road trips. We laughed, sang, and had fun all the way to Atlantic Beach. When we arrived at his friend's house, it was dark outside. I could smell the ocean and hear the waves, and if Aunt Terri had let me, I would have run straight into the water. I would have to wait until morning to dip my toes, and it felt just like Christmas Eve waiting for Santa to bring all the presents for you to open the next day. While Aunt Terri was getting dinner ready, I pestered Uncle Jim until he took me down to the shore so I could feel the water rush over my feet. That would have to do until tomorrow, and it was enough. After we ate, we sat on the screened in porch and listened to the waves. It was so relaxing that I fell asleep and the next thing I knew, Uncle Jim was carrying me to bed.

When I woke up the next morning, I couldn't wait to get on the beach. Aunt Terri made me eat a quick breakfast which delayed my fun. Uncle Jim and I both raced out the back door, down the stairs and onto the sand. I had my beach bag with Kool-Aid, Bugles and Twizzlers. Aunt Terri made me take some water which she wanted me to drink, but I planned on using it to wash the sand from my feet. The first thing I wanted to do was jump in the water, and Uncle Jim came with me. We splashed and played and swam for hours. Aunt Terri stayed on shore reading a book under an umbrella. After lunch, Uncle Jim was tired, so he wanted to take a nap, and since I still had plenty of energy I asked if I could bury him in the sand. Uncle Jim agreed, and I went to work. I read about doing this one time in a magazine and wanted to do it ever since. Now that I had my chance, I was going to make sure it was right. As he lay snoring in the sun, I buried Uncle Jim up to his neck. Aunt Terri watched between reading her book and laughed and laughed. She made sure to take pictures which she said she would use to black-mail him later. He woke up saying he had to use the bathroom, and he couldn't move. Uncle Jim was hoppin' mad when Aunt Terri wouldn't let me dig him out. She thought it was funny, but he sure didn't. When he finally got free, he ran into the house to use the bathroom cursing the whole time. Aunt Terri had to fix him a drink and promise to cook a special seafood dinner before he calmed down.

That night Aunt Terri cooked lobster and fried shrimp, which was Uncle Jim's favorite dinner. She made a salad, boiled corn, and fried some hush puppies, too. We never ate lobster at home, so this was a special treat. I asked Aunt Terri if I could help with dinner, but she said she needed to cook this dinner by herself to make up with Uncle Jim. By the look on his face, the dinner worked. I wasn't a big fan of lobster, but I killed the shrimp. After I cleaned the kitchen, I asked if we could take a walk on the beach. Aunt Terri and Uncle Jim held hands as they strolled down the beach. I hung back pretending to collect seashells with a flashlight so they could have their privacy. I liked watching them act like teenagers, and it felt nice to hear them doing grown folks' business that night when they went to bed. It made me feel safe and that was what I needed the most.

That trip was one to remember, and I did not want to leave the beach house. I loved that place, and one day when I am grown and have a husband, we will buy a house on the beach like this one to visit in the summer. I dreamed sweet dreams lying in the bed with the windows open, smelling the aroma of the sea and tasting the salt from the water on my lips when I licked them. We had the best time as a family, and Aunt Terri took plenty of pictures so we could remember the trip in days to come. I wrote in my journal most of the way home about how renewed I felt after visiting the ocean; it seemed to breathe a new life in me, and I was ready to take on anything. I realized watching my aunt and uncle, it's not love that hurts; it's the denial of love that hurts. Thanks to them, I was no longer hurting.

Chapter 21: Fifth Grade Blues

That beach trip was the last event of the summer, and I was ready to start at my new school and meet my new teacher. I hoped this year I wouldn't have any issues and that my teacher was nice. The first day of school I was really nervous and did not want to ride the bus. I dreamed the night before about the day Mr. Samuels attacked me. That was the last time I was on a bus, and I was afraid to go out alone. Since I got home from the hospital I had never been by myself; Aunt Terri, Vivi or Uncle Jim were with me wherever I went. Now I would leave the safety of my family and ride the bus alone. Sure, there would be other children and a bus driver, but I was not friends with any of them. What if something happened to me? No one would know who to contact. How would Aunt Terri find me if I got lost? Nobody knew my name. I got so upset that I broke out in hives, and boy, did they itch. I couldn't control myself, and I kept scratching and scratching. The hives turned into big red whelps all over my body. I looked a sight, and I did not want to go to school looking that way. Aunt Terri wasn't having it.

"Butterfly, you cannot miss the first day of school. Your teacher would never forgive me. Plus you don't want to get off on the wrong foot now, do you?" she asked. "I guess not, but look at me. Those kids will eat me alive!" I replied. "Well, let's see what we can do about that. Now hives are coming because you are nervous. What if I told you that all the other kids are just as nervous as you? Did you know the first day of school is one of the most stressful days of the year for both teachers and students?" Aunt Terri tried to comfort me. "You mean my teacher is scared, too?" I said with surprise. "Of course, I am a college professor, and I still get nervous before teaching my first class of the semester. Teachers are humans, too. You have to think of people as individuals. Everyone has the same fears as you. Everyone gets nervous or scared, but each person reacts to their feelings differently. You hold your fear inside and break out in hives, someone else may talk a lot, another person may sit quietly and watch everyone, while another person may get angry and lash out."

Everything Aunt Terri said made perfect sense to me. I felt better knowing the other kids were just like me, and my hives were starting to go down. I still did not want to ride the bus, so I asked Aunt Terri, "Will you please take me to school today so I won't have to ride the bus?" She said, "I thought you were getting too big to have someone take you to school. Don't you want to ride the bus with the rest of the kids?" I didn't want her to think I was a baby, but I was afraid, and I needed her. "Aunt Terri, I thought you would want to meet my new teacher and see my new classroom. I am going to a new school this year. How will you know where to come get me?" I think she could tell I needed her to take me, so she gave in without a fight. "OK Butterfly, I will take you today, but tomorrow you're on your own." That is all I wanted to hear. Tomorrow I would worry about another excuse for her to take me to school and pick me up, but today I was set.

As we arrived at the front of the school, I read the sign out front that said: "Welcome 5th Graders!" The teachers were all outside on the sidewalk to greet us, and they had signs with their names so we would know who they were and where to go. My teacher was named Mr. Brown, and he was there, too. Mr. Brown looked very mean, and I wasn't sure if I would like him. He was a very short, chubby man with gray hairs growing in his beard and on the side of his low cut hair. Mr. Brown had smooth chocolate skin that glowed in the morning sunlight, and he wore old man glasses on the tip of his nose. As soon as our eyes locked, I could tell he was not to be messed with. He smiled broadly and was very welcoming "Good morning, young lady. My name is Mr. Brown, and may I ask your name?" "Yes sir, my name is Zora Langston, and I am very happy to meet you," I answered. He seemed pleased that I was polite, and he shook my hand. "Well, Miss Zora, if you would please join the rest of the class over there, and as soon as everyone has arrived we will all walk to the classroom together," he directed. Aunt Terri introduced herself, and we walked over to the area labeled for Mr. Brown's class. There were kids with their parents, and then there were kids that rode the bus. We all stood around looking nervous while the parents chatted.

A little girl with freckles and red hair in pig tails walked up to me and introduced herself. Her name was Mary Jane and she was 10 also. Mary Jane was very friendly and informed me that we were going to be best friends. She was very nice, but a little too pushy for my liking. I have never been one who liked being told what to do, and it rubbed me the wrong way that she was taking away my choice in the matter of friendship. I decided I better keep my eye on her in case she was up to something. Mary Jane was a big talker, and she almost never shut up. This was a little annoying, and I immediately wanted to distance myself from her. Just because I was quiet and reserved did not mean I wanted someone around me talking all of the time. I welcomed silence and enjoyed sitting alone sorting through my own thoughts. With her around I couldn't hear myself think. I was thankful when we went to our classroom and Mary Jane's assigned seat was across the room from me. I just met her 10 minutes ago and already needed a break from her. Something told me she wasn't going to be my best friend, but then I thought about what Aunt Terri told me earlier. Maybe Mary Jane was just nervous, and she was very chatty as a result. I decided I would observe her for the rest of the week and make my decision then.

Our classroom was nicely decorated with bright colors and all kinds of pictures. There was a bulletin board on the wall with a border on it, but the center was blank. Mr. Brown said that he wanted the class to decorate the board twice a month. He said there would be contests, and the person who won would get to decorate the board. I was so excited because I loved arts and crafts, and I knew just what I would put on the board when my turn came. I couldn't wait for the first contest to begin. The first day of school was going fine until we had to tell the class about ourselves, our parents and what we did this summer. I decided I did not want my classmates to know all of my business so I would only tell them what I wanted them to know. I would talk about Aunt Terri and Uncle Jim and tell them about my trips to Carowinds and the beach. Nobody needed to know about my assault and the fact that Teresa Langston was in jail for trying to kill me. I knew it was a small town, but I did not think anyone in my class would know about it. Even if they knew, most people had the common decency to keep their mouth shut and not try to embarrass me. I did not have any enemies my age, so I did not see a reason anyone would try to pick on me. I had to come up with a plan just in case someone tried to pick a fight with me. Aunt Terri made it clear if I got in any more fights, I would have to go back to see the therapist-something I did not want to ever do again.

When my turn came to tell who I was and what I did this summer, I heard a couple of girls giggle in the back of the room and say, "This should be good." "My name is Zora Langston, and I turned 10 this summer. I love to read. My father passed away earlier this year, and I now live with my aunt and uncle. This summer I went to Carowinds in Charlotte and Myrtle Beach, South Carolina." The girls in the back kept on giggling and talking. "Tell us about how your mom tried to kill you and how her boyfriend took advantage of you," one girl called out. I froze and did not say anything. I wanted to cry, and I felt the tears welling up in my eyes when I remembered I promised myself I would not cry anymore. By this time the whole class was buzzing, and everyone was looking at me including, Mr. Brown. I stood up to face my new enemies and saw it was a girl that was on the VBS bus. She was one of the mean girls who caused me to run into the park that day. I thought she was older than me so, she must have been left back a year. Well, I was not afraid of her, and I had nothing to lose because I did not have any friends anyway.

"I wasn't going to discuss those topics, but since you brought it up, I will tell you," I said coldly. The room went silent, and the mean girls wiped the smiles off of their faces. I guess they thought I would cry and run away, but everything that happened to me this past year made me tough, and I no longer ran from a challenge. "Let's see, after my daddy died, my mom moved her boyfriend into our house. After a while he started making me do sex things with him, and eventually he attacked me in the park. He almost killed me after he violated my body, and I spent days in the hospital. My mom blamed me for him getting killed, and she tried to drown me at Mina Weil Pool. She is now in jail waiting for her trial. Did I leave anything out? Do you want to hear about how that man almost ruined me and how I fought for my life? Do you need all of the details or is that enough?" I was so mad I could spit fire, but I kept my calm and stared that girl right in the eye. She avoided looking at me, but I stood there for a good minute or two before Mr. Brown interceded and had me sit down. The entire class was looking down at their feet, and nobody wanted to look at me. Mr. Brown decided we needed a break and told everyone to go out for recess. He asked me to stay behind so we could chat.

"Zora, I had no idea you were the little girl I read about in the newspaper this summer. How have you been dealing with this tragedy in your life?" he asked. "I am taking it day by day, Mr. Brown.

My aunt and uncle are great people, and they fill the house with a lot of love, and they talk to me so I can express myself. My uncle started me writing a journal, and it has helped also. Mostly I pray, and God has helped me to put the bad things out of my mind so I can focus on all of the good things that have happened," I answered. "How have your friends reacted to you because of this?" he asked. "To be honest, I don't have any friends. My daddy was my best friend and now that he's dead, I really don't have any. My aunt and uncle are more like parents, so they aren't my friends, and I spend most of my time reading. The characters in my books are my friends, and I try to spend as much time as possible with them. Kids my age don't seem to like me. It's always been that way, so I can't blame it on what happened to me," I explained. Mr. Brown had this really sad look on his face, and he told me I could go outside to play. I chose to sit in the classroom to avoid the millions of questions I would surely get on the playground. I was finished with this subject, and I had no intention of reopening the conversation.

After recess, everyone went to the cafeteria to eat lunch. When I walked into the café, all of the kids turned to look at me. Apparently, my story had circulated all over the school, and I was now the alien with two heads. My stomach was doing flip flops, but I decided to just hold my head high and continue through the lunch line. Uncle Jim said to never let them see your weakness or they will take advantage of you, and he was right. I kept a stone face and decided this would be my way of getting through the day. Nobody would dare mess with me if I looked mean and crazy, so I kept that look on my face whenever I felt threatened. People moved out of my way as I walked, and I liked the way it felt to have this power. I thought to myself, "They might talk about me behind my back, but I do not have to worry about anyone messing with me to my face." Boy was I wrong! As soon as I sat down at the table to eat, the mean girl came up to me with her little friends in tow. She wanted to know what it was like to be assaulted by a man. I did not want to talk to her or her friends, so I tried to ignore them, but she would not be ignored. That little witch took her pudding and dumped it in my hair.

I just sat there, looking stupid with pudding on my head. Mr. Brown saw what happened and came to my rescue. I found out the mean girl was named Cynthia, and she was in big trouble. Mr. Brown was mad as fire and made her and her friends stay after school for detention. One of the lady teachers took me to the bathroom, and tried to wash the pudding out of my hair. Luckily, Aunt Terri had taken my hair out of the braids I wore all summer, and my hair was pulled back in a pony tail. It was easy to get the pudding out with this hair style, but if I had my braids it may have been impossible. For the rest of the day I sat quietly in my desk listening, but not participating in any of the class activities. I wanted to cry really badly, but I refused to let Cynthia have the upper-hand. I would say a prayer for her tonight, so she would be happier. I just couldn't figure out why she was attacking me and she didn't even know me. What had I done to her? Would it always be this way between us? I would have to find a way to either avoid her or make friends because we had a long way to go before we graduated. Maybe Aunt Terri could shed some light on how I could get along with her. I would much rather fight her and get it over with, but that would be the easy way out, and Aunt Terri would send me to the shrink.

When Aunt Terri came to pick me up from school, she was hit with a surprise. Mr. Brown walked me to the car and asked if he could speak to her for a minute. Immediately she thought I was in trouble and gave me a mean look. Aunt Terri got out of the car and spoke with Mr. Brown, but when she came back she was fire hot! "Zora, who is this Cynthia girl that decided to pick on you today?" she demanded. "I don't really know her, but she goes to our church. She was on the VBS bus that day," I recalled. "Well, I am very proud of you for not fighting her. She is just trying to establish her territory at school, and you were a threat to her. She had to make it known to her flunkies not to like you. She tried to embarrass you, and when that didn't work she resorted to violence. She is a simple girl, and I don't want you to give her the time of day. Eventually she will leave you alone and find someone else to target," Aunt Terri chimed. "Aunt Terri, I can't avoid her because she sits right behind me. What am I supposed to do tomorrow when she tries to fight me? I heard her telling her friends that she was going to whoop my tail after school tomorrow because she got detention." I did not know what to do, and Aunt Terri was no help. She thought of things like a college professor, not a 5th grader. Girls like Cynthia did not want to talk; she would not stop until I fought her. She was the type of girl who had to rule the school, and she needed people to be afraid of her to do that. Eventually I would have to fight her if I wanted to continue going to this school. 5th grade rules were not like adult rules, and she was out to get me. I would just pray about it, and I knew God would lead me out of this situation. All I knew was the first day of school was hard, and it wasn't going to get any easier for me. This was going to be an interesting school year.

Chapter 22: Love Me or Leave Me Alone

When Uncle Jim came home that night he knew something was wrong immediately. Aunt Terri did not have to say a word. He asked me, "Babygirl, what happened at school today?" All of a sudden I felt relieved that I could talk to him about Cynthia. "Uncle Jim, this girl at school decided she wanted to make me her target, and poured pudding on my head when I did not fight her," I said. "That doesn't sound like the whole story. What else happened?" he asked. "Okay, so our teacher, Mr. Brown asked us to introduce ourselves and tell what we did this summer. When my turn came I told them my name, and that I lived with my aunt and uncle because my daddy is dead. I also told them about our trips to Carowinds and Myrtle Beach. Just as I was finishing up, things went wrong. This older girl sitting in the back of the room said something about my mom being in jail for trying to kill me....," I informed him.

The more I talked the more I could see Uncle Jim getting hot under the collar. I told him the whole story and waited for him to explode. "This little girl is threatened by you. She must see how special you are and wants to make sure all of the other kids stay away from you. People like her try to dull your shine, and since she is unhappy she is trying to make you that way, too. They say misery loves company. Here's what you do: try to avoid this girl, but if she so much as breathes on you I want you to knock the stuffing out of her." Aunt Terri objected, but Uncle Jim continued, "Those little girls are lions, and Cynthia is the pride leader, the alpha female. The rest of the pride will not know what to do if you take out their leader. In the wild, lions fight for the top spot in the pride, and once it's established the only way to lose it is to have a younger lion take it by force. I want you to be that younger lion. Take her out, and the other girls will follow you. Girls that age don't know what loyalty is yet. They follow the leader blindly." Uncle Jim sounded like the man on Mutual of Omaha's Wild Kingdom talking about prides and lions. I listened to what he was saying, but wasn't sure I would be able to lead a pride of 5th grade girls when I didn't even have one friend.

Cynthia was a main concern for me, and I needed to be ready for her. I knew she would try to get me when there were no adults around, and the bus would be the perfect place. She and her girls could have me cornered with nowhere to go, and I needed to avoid this at all costs. I thought about how I could plot and scheme to get Aunt Terri to take me to school every day. I could try to trick her like I did on the first day of school, but I decided that being sneaky was not for me, so I went right up to Aunt Terri and said, "I don't want to ride the bus." "Butterfly, what do you mean? What's wrong with riding the bus?" Aunt Terri replied. "Every time I ride the bus something bad happens. I don't want to be attacked anymore," I exclaimed. Aunt Terri was silent for a moment, and she looked helplessly over at Uncle Jim with tears in her eyes. Uncle Jim stopped reading his paper and came over on the couch where I was sitting. "Babygirl, what do you mean by that?" he said quietly. He looked very sad and almost defeated. "The last time I was on the bus coming home from church I had problems with the kids and then it broke down which meant I had to walk. I ended up walking through the park, and Mr. Samuels attacked me. I just don't want that to happen again." I heard my voice crack as I spoke, and I wanted it to be over. Why does Aunt Terri need an explanation for everything? Why can't she just listen to my request and then agree to it? This whole time I was looking down at my shoes because I did not want to see the judgment and the guilt on their faces. Whenever I talked about what happened in the park, they always looked at me with this weird kind of "it's your fault" kind of look. Then it always changed to a guilty look like it was their fault. The truth was there were only two people responsible for this mess; one was dead, and the other was in jail. When I looked up from my shoes, I saw that Aunt Terri was crying, and Uncle Jim had tears in his eyes. I wondered if they would ever get over letting me go to VBS that day. The guilt they felt was written all over their faces and I had to do something to make them feel better. "Aunt Terri, please don't cry. I'm sorry I asked about the bus. I will just suck it up and ride the bus," I said while moving over to Aunt Terri's chair to give her a big hug. I hated to see her cry, and all of this could have been avoided if I had just faced my fears. "You will do nothing of the sort. If my Butterfly feels uncomfortable riding the bus, then I will take her to school," Aunt Terri exclaimed. "Terri, what about when your classes at the college start? What are you going to do then?" Uncle Jim asked. "We will find a way, Jim. I'm not going to let this child ride the bus if she feels scared like that. I will just have to re-schedule my classes to start around 9:00 am instead of 8:00 am, so I can make it there on time. I'll speak to the dean about it, and I'm sure it can be arranged." It was settled, round one to Zora. Cynthia and her crew could not beat me up if I wasn't on the bus.

The next couple of weeks at school went pretty well because Cynthia and her friends were still being punished in detention. They did not want to extend their punishment so they were on their best behavior. I knew this would eventually change, and I needed to watch my back. The other kids in the class were friendlier than Cynthia, and I was able to get along just fine. Even Mary Jane seemed to have calmed down and wasn't talking so much. She and I had become friendlier, but I was still a little cautious where she was concerned.

Mr. Brown was proving to be a good teacher, and he made class fun. We were always doing crafts and science projects, and he even introduced music to the class. Everyone was learning how to play the flute-o-phone, and we were reading music, too. I knew I couldn't sing, and I loved music so I decided that playing an instrument was the way to go. I just knew I was going to be great. We practiced every day in class and Mr. Brown said we were coming along. I could play the flute-o-phone by ear, but I had a hard time reading the music notes. It all looked like gibberish, and I could barely tell one from the other. I was very confused and could not understand why I was having so much trouble reading the notes. I considered myself a pretty smart girl, and I read words like nobody's business. Why couldn't I read these music notes? I was ashamed, and instead of asking for help, I decided to learn the music by ear so I could keep up in class and nobody would know. That's exactly what I did, every day I practiced at home after school. You would have thought I was in training to play with the NC Orchestra. I worked so hard at learning to play by ear that I even fooled myself; that is until Mr. Brown announced that we were going to have a recital for our parents and I was to have a solo. Was he crazy? I was not going to play this thing in front of people, not by myself with everyone staring at me. I almost passed out when he said that. There were to be three featured soloists, and it was a big deal. At least I did not have to learn any new songs, but I felt like a fraud because all of the other soloists could read music. I had gotten a little better, and I could follow along with the few songs we played, but if he asked me to read music from a different song I would be lost. I lived in fear that someone would notice, and then everyone would laugh at me. I knew music was not my thing, but Uncle Jim was so proud that I was able to play any instrument that he started saying I was going to be a star. He could sing like nobody's business and he played the piano and bass guitar, but he never learned to read music. He was so happy that I was learning and wanted me to start teaching him. I kept avoiding giving him lessons by saying that I needed to practice for my solo. "My Babygirl is reading music! I am so proud of you and as soon as that concert is over I am lining up for my first lesson. I can't wait to see you up on that stage. You are gonna be great, and I will be right down front cheering." Uncle Jim was over the moon with excitement, which just made me feel more pressure. "That's great, Uncle Jim. May I go to my room and practice now? I don't want to mess up with you being in the audience," I lied. I did not care if he was in the audience or not. I knew I was going to mess up and be ridiculed. I just knew it.

As if trying to keep up with this music class wasn't enough, Vivi came over with news about Teresa Langston's trial. "Zora your mother's trial is set to begin next week. The prosecutor tried everything he knew to avoid you having to testify, but the judge did not go for it. You will be called as a witness in this case. This means you will have to take an oath, get up in front of the entire courtroom, and explain what happened to the jury." I was scared and did not want to do it. "What do you mean I have to? I thought you said I would never have to talk about it again if I didn't want to. I can't do it. I won't!" I screamed. Vivi was clearly upset and tried to calm me down "Listen, Zora. I know you must be very afraid. I can't imagine having my own mother try to kill me and then being asked to testify in front of a bunch of people about what happened. This will be one of the hardest things you will ever have to do, but I have faith that you can do it. Do you want her out on the streets again? You know she will be gunning for you as soon as her feet hit the pavement. You have to put an end to this torture she is subjecting you to. I know you can do this," Vivi tried to reassure me. I did not want to disappoint her, and I knew what she was saying was right, but I was still scared. What if they didn't believe me? What if she killed me in the courtroom? All she would have to do is take the gun from the cops and shoot me before anyone could stop her. For the first time in my life I knew what might happen to me before it happened, and I was not ready to die. Sure I wanted to see Daddy and Grandma Rose again, but not quite so soon. "Babygirl, you can do this. All you have to do is go up there put your hand on the Bible and tell the truth. The judge will be there, so the lawyers can't do anything to you. Aunt Terri and I will be outside waiting for you and the police will be there to protect you from your mom. You will be just fine. If you're super scared, all you have to remember is God is there to protect you. He knows everything you've been through, and I know He doesn't want you to hurt anymore." Uncle Jim always had a way of making things clear for me. I calmed down and decided that if I could do this, then dealing with Cynthia would be a breeze. The rest of the week I spent my time after school practicing for the recital and preparing for the trial. Vivi brought the prosecutor over to our house, and he asked me several questions about what happened at the pool. He told me about how Teresa Langston's lawyer would try to trick me, and we practiced some of the questions he might ask as well. I was ready for the trial, but I would have to miss school on that day. Aunt Terri had to testify also, but she would be called separately from me.

The day of the trial I was very nervous, but I was ready to tell what happened. I could not go into the courtroom until my name was called, so Vivi sat outside in the hall with me. When the man called my name, I felt my stomach drop. I looked at Vivi, and she smiled and told me I would be fine. I walked into the courtroom, and it was nothing like what I remember from *To Kill a Mockingbird*. The only thing that was similar was the fact that the judge sat up high and there were people in the jury box. There were flags behind the judge, one for the United States and one for the state of North Carolina. As I walked toward what Vivi called the stand, I felt everyone's eyes burning on my skin. They acted like they had never seen a little black girl before. Just then I saw her. There she was, Teresa Langston staring at me with her dead eyes. She was not happy to see me and her energy was mean and angry. The prosecutor told me she would probably try to intimidate me and to avoid looking at her, but as soon as I made eye contact with her, I couldn't look away. She stared at me, and I stared back at her. If she was trying to scare me, it did not work. I was no longer afraid, and I knew I had to be strong. This time she was not getting away with her mess. I was going to make sure she went away for a very long time.

I took the oath on the Bible, and that reminded me that God was there to protect me. I took the stand and answered all of the prosecutor's questions. He asked things about my life growing up with Teresa Langston, about my daddy's death, and about Mr. Samuels. The defense attorney objected a few times, but the judge overruled him. I made sure to tell the complete truth in great detail just like the prosecutor told me. By the time I finished some of the ladies in the jury box were crying and the men looked shocked and sad. The defense attorney must have seen that too because he was very nice to me and only asked a few questions. At first I avoided looking at Teresa Langston, but the more I talked, the more confident I became. I stared her right in the eyes as I told the family secrets for everyone to hear. She became uncomfortable and hung her head. It was now her who was avoiding my eyes. I knew at that moment that I would never be bothered by her again. She may have tried to kill me, but she failed, and that was my strength. I could survive anything now, and I knew it. All of a sudden facing Cynthia and her crew did not seem so hard.

I finished testifying, and Uncle Jim took me home. Aunt Terri had to stay because she still had to take the stand. I was happy to be finished, and Uncle Jim seemed relieved. As a treat we stopped at Dairy Queen and got a cone. I got a chocolate vanilla swirl, and Uncle Jim got chocolate. We sat outside under a tree and ate our ice cream and talked a little. "I was real proud of you today, Babygirl. You were so strong, and the way you spoke it was like you were not scared. That jury should have an easy time convicting your mom after hearing everything that happened to you. How do you feel about what's happening?" he asked. "Well, at first I was scared, especially when I first saw her and the way she was looking at me. Once I started talking I realized I had the upper hand, and if I did a good job, she would be put away. Do you really think they will lock her up for good?" I asked. "I can't be sure, but I know if I was on that jury there would be no question. Now I want you to remember that she is on trial for attempted murder, so even if she is convicted, she will not be in there for the rest of her life. She will eventually get out depending on her sentence, and one day she may try to contact you," he warned. "I'm fine, Uncle Jim, and even if she only spends a few years in jail, it should be long enough for her to think about what she tried to do to me, and maybe she will repent." Uncle Jim looked at me and shook his head. He had a small smile on his face, and he seemed pleased. We went home to cook dinner for Aunt Terri because she would be tired after her long day in court.

Now that I was finished with the trial, I went back to concentrating on my solo. I practiced very hard and had perfected every song. I still couldn't read music like I wanted, but I could read enough to get by. A few days before the recital, there was quite a stir in our classroom. Some of the teachers heard that the verdict was in for the Teresa Langston trial. I didn't know what a verdict was, but I guessed they made a decision about her going to jail. All of the adults were buzzing about it during lunch and I overheard a few teachers talking. Apparently it was the talk of the town, and the teachers were gossiping like hens. As soon as we returned to our classroom, Cynthia started in on me. "Look at her just sitting there like nothing is wrong. She snitched on her own mother and put her in jail. In my neighborhood you don't snitch! People take care of each other, and if something bad happens, the neighbors take care of it." Her friend Jane chimed in, "You know she ain't from the projects. She don't have that loyalty like we do in Westhaven. She wouldn't last a day in out part of town. She lives in a nice pretty house, and she has sweet little tea parties." They all laughed and thought it was funny to talk about the most painful part of my life. None of them had been through anything close to what I was going through, and they never would. I chose to ignore them instead of getting sucked into their issues. I didn't know anybody who would let someone who tried to kill them go free, not even in the projects. Before the girls could get going again, there was a knock on the door. Mr. Brown asked for me to come out into the hall and to bring my stuff. Aunt Terri was there to take me home. She wanted to talk about the trial and thought it would be better for me to leave school for the day. When we got home, Uncle Jim and Vivi were waiting for me. I thought for sure they were going to tell me that Teresa Langston was set free, but they said she was found guilty. She was sentenced to 20 years in prison with the possibility of parole in 12 years. Aunt Terri explained that parole meant if she was good in prison she could possibly get out in 12 years, but not before. I would be 22 years old before she could possibly be released. I was both sad and relieved that she was being placed in prison. She would be transported to the state penitentiary in Raleigh, and I would not have to see her again. I wondered if she missed Queenie and Big Willie. What would happen to them now that their mom was going to prison for a very long time?

The day before the big recital I was very excited. During class we had one last practice, and then it was time to perform. Aunt Terri put my hair in afro puffs that day because she planned on braiding my hair for the recital, and she wanted them to be fresh. Everyone had to wear black bottoms and white tops with black shoes. I was going to wear my butterfly necklace for good luck, and Uncle Jim was bursting at the seams. Tomorrow couldn't come fast enough.

I was sitting at my desk studying my music notes when all of a sudden Cynthia and her crew surrounded me. The time had come for me to defend myself, and this time I would not back down. Cynthia started in again about me being a snitch, and out of nowhere she pulled out a pair of scissors and cut one of my puffs clean off my head. I couldn't believe this crazy girl had cut my hair. In my world she may as well have spit in my face. "Nobody cuts my hair!" I screamed as I picked up my bottle of glue and smashed her across the face. I didn't give her time to react; I took the scissors from her hand and cut her shirt off. I smashed her in the face so hard with my fist that her nose immediately started bleeding. I wailed on her as I heard Jane and Cherie say, "That girl is crazy, I ain't messin' with her," as they ran off. By the time Mr. Brown pulled me off of her, Cynthia looked like Rocky Balboa after Apollo Creed fought him in *Rocky*. I was in control the entire time, not like the time I fought Queenie. I had a plan, and it was being executed exactly as I had drawn it up. I attacked the alpha lioness and damaged her so badly that no one in their right mind would follow her. I was taking over as the leader of this pride, and I would rule with kindness and acceptance. The other lionesses would fall in line behind me because they saw my takeover move. From this point on, no one would mistreat Zora Langston ever again!

ABOUT THE AUTHOR

LISA W. TETTING IS THE CREATOR OF REBIRTHOFLISA, HER PERSONAL BLOG. SHE IS A FORMER CALL CENTER SUPERVISOR, WHO, AFTER MUCH THOUGHT AND ANGST, DECIDED TO CHANGE HER LIFE BY LIVING HER DREAM. *THE MISTREATMENT OF ZORA LANGSTON* IS HER FIRST NOVEL. SHE GREW UP IN A SMALL TOWN IN NORTH CAROLINA AND LOVES THAT SHE IS A SOUTHERN GIRL. SHE HAS BEEN HAPPILY MARRIED TO HER WONDERFUL HUSBAND FOR A LITTLE OVER 14 YEARS, AND THEY CURRENTLY RESIDE IN TAMPA, FLORIDA.